WHITE WALLS

KATIE OSTROVECKY

Cynthia,

Thank you for your support!

Katie

Editor: Jared Windt
Cover Photography: Stephanie Romero

Dedicated to anyone who has needed help finding the light.

WHITE WALLS

White Walls is based on a true story. Names, dates, and some places have been changed to protect those in the book.

PART ONE

Kayleigh

Gray. The color of her eyes that cautiously studied me as I walked into the room. Her eyes showed sadness and pain while her body seemed tired and defeated. I had done this a million times before, but something felt different yet so very familiar at the same time. It had been 10 years since I took a case back at this hospital and it felt as if nothing had changed.

The hallways were still a bland shade of cream white and decorations were scarce. The lack of welcoming warmth was chilling. Every door. Every room. So much monotony. The bright lighting added to my discomfort as I'd walked through the building earlier. The workers put on a smile for me, but I knew how cold they could be. As one of them led me into the room, I prepared myself for what was to come.

Vanessa was a 23 year old female who had been admitted a little over 48 hours ago. I read her files over and over again, trying to put the pieces of her story together. She was a bright young lady. A college graduate with outstanding grades. A competitive athlete. And, now, a full-time job working in sports medicine. From my understanding, her father flew across the country when she had been admitted. Therefore, it seemed like she had some family support as well.

What I couldn't understand was why this beautiful, driven young lady was sitting in front of me today. Her files stated she was contemplating suicide and her behavior was erratic and borderline dangerous. I yearned to learn this young lady's story, but I knew it would take a lot of time and even more patience...

Vanessa

Dark blue. The color I use to describe this feeling. It's as if the whole world is collapsing on you and the darkness begins to consume you. It starts with your thoughts and then it works its way into your bones, paralyzing all control you once had. Sinking into the dark blue, like drowning in an ocean, unable to stay afloat.

I wish these walls were dark blue. At least that would be more appealing than these off-white walls. Gosh, this place was depressing. Ha. How ironic. Funny how God throws in these ironic moments (if "he" even exists). When I began questioning my faith... I don't even know. Maybe it was when I found out the lies, or maybe when I sat on my bed with a gun to my head. Forty-eight hours ago I was ready to believe that this was it. No heaven, no hell, or maybe I was currently living in it. It sure felt like it. The only thing I knew for sure was that I needed to get out of here.

I'm exhausted right now and the last thing I want is more meetings with random people who just want to "help" me. My dad told me to sleep it off while I'm stuck in here, but that's nearly impossible when the workers are coming to your room every hour of the night to make sure you haven't disappeared. I have considered stealing one of their badges and escaping this place in the night. When they let people go outside for smoke breaks I spotted a gate I could climb and jump over if I really wanted to.

Kayleigh. That's my social worker's name. She looks nice enough, but so did everyone else when I first checked in. They "look nice," but none of them have helped me. In all honesty, they all look miserable like they despise their jobs. Kayleigh has a look of sincerity in her eyes and I'm hoping she can get me some answers as to how I can get the fuck out of here. Apparently her and my doctor are the ones who give me the clearance to get out of this shit hole. And, seeing as my doctor was quite the pompous asshole to me yesterday, Kayleigh is my only hope.

The psychiatrist. Where do I even start with him? I was actually excited to meet with him and get some help... until he went on the offensive and spoke to me as if I were a child. After I figured out he had no respect for me I zoned out and his words quickly became a repetitive "blah, blah, blah" to me. That was until I heard him explaining the medications he was prescribing me. Despite my frustration, I politely explained to him that I don't believe in taking medications for my current condition.

"Vanessa – I don't think you understand. The longer you refuse your pills, the longer it will take for you to be released."

I'm not going to lie. I was furious. Not only am I suicidal, imprisoned, and scared but, now, I am being threatened to take medication I don't want to take. My road to freedom seemed nonexistent at this point. I thought these people were here to help me, not trick me and treat me as if I am dumb. This place makes me feel crazy, and more depressed.

Luckily, two more hours until visitor time. I can't wait to see my dad and escape from these suffocating white walls for an hour.

Kayleigh

Well, I guess that meeting could have been worse, but it also could have gone better. The first meeting is always the toughest for me. I know that my patients are looking to me for help, and although I try to help them, they usually end up feeling betrayed by me. I know she wants to get out, but can't Vanessa see that she isn't ready?

She is so lost and my heart aches for her. I wish she knew how much I truly care and how much I truly want to help her get back to her normal life. I know this process isn't easy though and she will probably get even more angered and frustrated with us. I wish I didn't have to be so stern, but I need to keep her safe and the only way I can do that is by keeping her here. Hopefully she can understand that soon.

The hardest part about this job is never knowing the whole truth. I've read the reports and listened to her story, but what really happened that day? What is the cause of her sadness and lack of will to live? So many unanswered questions that I may never know the truth about.

She says that she is okay and that she is ready to go home, but that's what they all say. This job is a dangerous game of Russian roulette. I could let her go home in hopes that she is better now, but I could also release her too early and get that dreaded phone call that she did something again and, this time, succeeded. I'm so scared. I can't lose another patient – not again.

So much for my social worker being on my side. Looks are deceiving – she's a bitch. Doesn't she know I'm fine? This whole system is so fucked up. I have no rights. How is this even legal? If my health insurance would stop covering my stay here, then they couldn't hold me any longer. Is it ironic that I wish I had shitty health insurance?

I feel really low today. I'm falling deeper into this world of dark blue. I started taking my medications today. They make me feel numb and they help me sleep. Anything to pass the time. I miss my bed, my dog, my job. I miss being able to eat good food. I don't know how many more cafeteria meals I can eat. I've already lost a lot of weight because I can't stomach a full meal and, even if I could, the food is so disgusting that I wouldn't want to. Dad says he'll take me to In-N-Out the day I get released. I can't wait.

I would kill for a cheeseburger right now. Oops. I take that back. Don't want these people to think I'm crazy or dangerous for saying I would "kill for a cheeseburger." The lady at the Urgent Psychiatric Care (UPC) actually accused me of endangering others.

"Vanessa – don't you know how dangerous it is to carry gun ammo in your purse?"

No, you idiot. I'm pretty sure bullets are only dangerous when they are inside the gun and I didn't even have the gun at the time. Doesn't matter though. She said that would be a big reason why they hold me here longer.

Talk about the worst 24 hours of my life, and no that is not an exaggeration. I wouldn't wish a stay at the UPC on my worst of enemies. You really think you've seen crazy... until you spend a night there. Imagine a room full of the craziest people you could think of and times that by ten – welcome to the UPC. I think I saw about three naked men and women along with multiple fights and racial slurs toward other patients and employees.

One guy kept yelling the "N" word at one of the employees and wouldn't stop until they tranquilized him with some sort of sleeping medication. These people were animals and the employees treated them as such. They even treated me that way. The women on each side of me kept trying to talk to me, but they were so fucked up on drugs that they couldn't put one coherent thought together.

The area they kept us in was a large open room called the "observation room." The psychiatrists', social workers', and nurses' offices were facing the room with a large glass window that allowed them to monitor our every move. Men and women shared this open space, each with their own handy-dandy reclining chair (which doubled as our beds as night). It was far from comforting knowing that I would have no privacy from the other mentally ill people around me.

It didn't take long for me to realize that people in this place were not like me. Most of them seemed to have intense drug problems – meth, coke, heroine. I had never seen this before. Other people had severe mental conditions (I'm assuming schizophrenia or a combination of diseases). I felt bad for them, but mostly I was terrified for myself. I didn't feel safe. Then the thought crossed my mind: Am I like them? Am I just as crazy?

I sobbed until my eyes were dry and no more tears would come out. I remember thinking, "Why God? Why am I here and where are you when I need you the most?" One of the male nurses stopped in front of my chair and asked me why I was crying. He then looked me up and down and said, "Why is a young girl like yourself here? Your life should be perfect." No shit, asshole. My life should be perfect. But I guess perfect lives lead to depression and suicide attempts, don't they?

Well, long story short, they finally told me I would be leaving the UPC... but not to go home. They told me I had to voluntarily accept to go to another hospital that would get me the help I need. Otherwise, they would send me to an institution out in the middle of the desert, making it difficult to ever have visitors. It was a no-brainer at the time, but now that I'm here at this hospital I feel like I was tricked into another scheme to trap me in this fucked up system.

Kayleigh

Any time a patient comes from the Urgent Psychiatric Care center they are usually a little messed up in the head. It's no place for a young, depressed girl to be. Unfortunately that's not how the state laws work. If someone thinks an individual is a danger to themselves then that person can call the cops, who are then obligated to take the individual to the UPC to be evaluated.

In Vanessa's case, her ex-boyfriend called the cops not knowing the state laws for mental health scenarios. From what he told me and what Vanessa told me, it was a pretty traumatic event for both of them. He told me that he didn't know what else to do to keep her safe. As this whole situation was unraveling, it is my understanding that Vanessa's father was booking a flight and on his way to Arizona from their home on the east coast. Everything happened so fast that I'm sure it was hard on her, her ex, and her father. However, I can't help but wonder what really happened between her and her ex to land her here in the mental hospital. It's not my place to judge, but I'm sure Vanessa was not completely guilty and I'm sure her ex-boyfriend was not completely innocent. Maybe our next meeting will give me a little more insight into what Vanessa was thinking that day.

Vanessa

It was a hot, humid summer day in southwest Virginia. Today was my first day as an intern with a big division one football program. I remember meeting him briefly as I was introduced, but didn't think much of it. I was so focused on my work that I must have missed the subtle attraction between the two of us.

I had just gotten out of a very unhealthy relationship, to say the least. My college boyfriend had cheated on me multiple times and I was stupid enough to forgive him every time. I still remember the drunken nights when he would be yelling at me in the club, in front of all of our friends. I kept telling myself it was just a phase... that we would work through it and he would grow up. Well, he didn't. But I did. I outgrew his childish ways and decided it was time to grow on my own.

Then I met him – my dream guy. A man of God who was kind, handsome, athletic, and everything I could ever hope for. I never thought I would find someone who loved me the way he did. He helped remind me of the worth I felt like I'd lost in my previous relationship. I honestly didn't even want to be in a relationship, but it was too perfect to ignore. I felt like it was God's way of telling me it was my time to be happy and get what I deserved.

After months of getting to know each other, we finally decided to start dating following my internship. Although we were dating long distance for the rest of the winter and spring, everything still came easy for us. So when he asked me to move across the country with him following graduation, it seemed like an easy decision. While I was hesitant at first, I promised him that I would make the move as long as I found a job before he moved out there (and I did).

It was an exciting time and I felt so blessed to finally find a man who treated me right. We would even pray together and read devotions which solidified my belief that he was the one for me. In my heart, I felt as if he was "the one" and I was finally done being abused and broken by another man.

I was wrong. You never know how badly someone can truly hurt you until the person you love the most betrays you. My head is spinning and my heart aches reliving that day in my head. I used to be filled with warmth, but I feel so cold now.

Kayleigh

I've noticed something really beautiful about Vanessa. She has been uplifting the other girls during her stay here. I'm not sure if it's her defense mechanism for dealing with her own issues, but she lights up the room when she is encouraging the other girls. I wonder if she even sees the beauty in her own actions and the positive ripples they create. I can tell she has a pure and loving heart, but this disease is deteriorating. Like so many before her, depression is destroying Vanessa from the inside out.

I was able to sit down and speak with her father this morning. He seems concerned, but surprisingly unemotional. His biggest concern is getting Vanessa out of the hospital, but I explained to him why it was so important for her to stay. I will say that he was pretty angered when he heard about the doctor threatening Vanessa to take the medications. I find "threatening" to be a bit of a stretch. I know that the psychiatrist can come across as harsh, but I also know that he cares. I spoke to him regarding the issue today so I'm hoping he softens up toward Vanessa. I have a group meeting with both of them tomorrow so I'll be mediating quite a bit.

I'm hoping we can all get on the same page regarding Vanessa's progress and her tentative release date. I know she isn't ready yet, but giving her a release date may help her get through the rest of her days here.

I hate them. Even after "progress" and a few days here they still won't let me leave. I wonder if I'll ever get out of this place and, when I do, if I'll even have a job anymore. It's hard to believe I lived a "normal" life before this. Full-time job, decent pay, and a beautiful home. I'm not sure what I will be coming home to after this. Will he be there? Will he allow me to come home? What will happen next?

Honestly, I'm more concerned about my kids right now (and no, not real kids). Working in the high school setting can be extremely stressful, but it is ten times more rewarding. I started my job at the high school six months ago and fresh out of college. I wasn't really excited because I felt like I was settling, but taking this job meant that I could be out in Arizona with my boyfriend. He practically begged me to move there with him and I was all for it — even though it meant turning down multiple graduate school acceptances.

Graduate school was always my plan following my undergraduate studies, but then I had new plans — we had new plans. I no longer thought about just my future, but now it was about our future. I knew that my boyfriend would need me during his first season playing professional football so I decided it was best for me to support his dreams. Mine could wait, right?

Wrong. I was finally starting to realize all the sacrifices I made for him and the lack of ones I made for myself. I quickly became complacent in order to adjust to his needs. I had put him first so many times that I didn't know what to do now. I'd forgotten how to take care of myself. How many more sacrifices would I have made for him if this hadn't happened? I'm afraid I would've lost myself. Although I'm pretty sure I already have.

Looking into the mirror right now all I see is darkness. I don't even recognize myself anymore. Pupils the size of pinpoints... I haven't seen them this small since I abused painkillers in high school. And don't even get me started on my hairy legs. They won't let me shave alone because we could use the razors to hurt ourselves. I guess that makes sense since I know a lot of girls cut themselves in here, but I seriously just want to have smooth legs again.

I hid a baggie of shower items in my room that we aren't supposed to have. Once again, they think we will hurt ourselves by swallowing too much shampoo or body soap. Is it a crime to want to stay clean? The rules around here are absolute bullshit. I feel like a child again and I'm stuck in a never-ending time out.

The one decent thing about this place is the recreation time we have every day. They allow us to work out if we want to. Granted, there are only a few pieces of equipment, but it's enough for me to shut my mind off for a little while. I've been dying to go on a long run outside. I wish I could be back home, able to walk out of my front door to the trails of my favorite park.

The day everything happened I ran around the park in hopes that it would push out the dark depressing thoughts. Five minutes into my run, the tears started flowing and my lungs constricted as all the emotions came back. When I got to the top of the mountain, I remember thinking to myself, "This is where I will end it." I wanted to be somewhere beautiful and serene, and, most importantly, secluded when I ended it.

I would do anything to be sitting on that mountain right now.

Kayleigh

I'm not sure if Vanessa is thinking too much or not thinking at all. Every time I see her she has this blank stare as if she has completely shut down and closed herself off. I mean, I can't blame her, but I wish I could get through to her.

The nurses told me that she uses the community phone every chance she gets. I hope she's using it to call people other than her ex-boyfriend. Sadly, she still has the hope that he will come visit her, but I'm not sure that is the best idea. I don't know if she is seeking closure, but if so, it's too early for her to find it.

Her father gave me a little more insight into Vanessa's past history dealing with depression and suicide. Apparently, she started showing signs, or "cries for help," when she was in high school. One time she even overdosed on painkillers and isolated herself from all of her friends and family for weeks. He said that was the first time him and his wife were aware that something more serious was going on. She went to counseling a few times, but it sounds like it fizzled out and everyone moved on. They always wanted to help her more, but they just didn't know how.

That's usually the case with most of these scenarios. The depressed individual usually has a support system, but no one really knows how to help. It is saddening to see the struggle that family and friends of these individuals go through. This disease rots through individuals, families, friends, and ultimately society. When will our nation realize that this epidemic is spreading and will continue to do so until we take action?

I don't think you actually know when it starts. First, it was just a few bumps in the road, a few low days. Then a few days become a few weeks and sometimes even a few months. Every good thought is consumed by a dark fog that rolls over the mind until the body succumbs to it.

So, when they ask me when the depression started, I don't really know how to respond. I noticed it in high school, but maybe those dark thoughts were planted in my head long before that. I tried to push the thoughts out of my head for the longest time. I thought I was a dramatic teenage girl and that I just needed to get my shit together. It would pass in time, or at least that's what I thought.

The first "episode" happened following my first big break-up (I know, how cliché). It was the summer between sophomore and junior year in high school. I didn't really know how to react the first time I had a dark thought. I was confused, scared, and unable to comprehend or deal with these new thoughts invading my mind.

No one knew how to help me. Some people were scared and others were angry, but none of them understood. I knew it would always be that way because, if they understood, that would mean they would have to experience it – that deep sadness and hopelessness. I wouldn't wish this disease on them, let alone on the worst of my enemies.

Following high school, I really thought those days were in the past. I was off to a new state, a new school, meeting new friends and creating a new life. But throughout college and wherever I went, I could never shake the feeling. I kept feeling a tug on my mind – the fog clouding my judgement and emotions – preventing me from attaining stability or complete happiness. I even went on and off different medications to help "balance" my chemically imbalanced mind. Nothing seemed to help.

I was just about ready to give up again during my sophomore year of college. I was an athletic training major assigned to the cross country team and consistently slammed with commitments to my school work, leadership organizations, and soccer team. If I had to listen to my assistant coach scream at me one more time I was going to fucking blow.

I remember sitting in my athletic trainer's office holding back tears as I explained to him my thoughts of suicide. I had been here before and the dreadful feeling felt oh so familiar. Except, this time, I sought out help immediately. He set me up with our sports psychologist who I met with a total of one time.

Soccer made me so unhappy that I ended up leaving the team. My coach was very supportive, but most of my teammates never understood. I can't hold that against them though considering none of them knew the real truth as to why I left the team. How could I tell them the truth and expect them to look at me the same? The one person who always stood by my side was my teammate, classmate, and best friend. Her positivity and understanding carried me through a lot of difficult lows during our college years. I wish I had her with me now.

School was the one thing I never gave up on. I threw all my energy into my school work and buried myself in research and assignments. As nerdy as it sounds, I loved learning and I especially loved my athletic training classes. My grades were the one thing I could control and I finally found something I was good at. I didn't have to compete with anyone except myself. I found so much joy in my athletic training rotations that I thought this could be the key to staying above water.

I wish I was at work with my athletes right now instead of in this hell. They give me purpose and right now I feel as if I have none. The longer I'm in here, the less purpose I feel like I have.

Kayleigh

Well, the good news is that we decided on a release date for Vanessa. The bad news is that it's not for another few days. She's not very happy about that, but at least she has something to look forward to. We've been setting up appointments following her release. She will meet with a therapist once a week and I'm hoping she takes it seriously this time around. Especially considering her immediate family lives across the country – she'll need all the support she can get.

Seven days in here may seem like a lifetime to Vanessa, but it's a small chunk of time in the bigger picture. I hope these seven days will be enough to change her mind. The last thing I want is to see her back in here, or worse – in a coffin.

Vanessa

I'm scared. Every day I'm stuck in here my mind goes to darker places. How am I supposed to get better when I'm trapped in my own mind all day? I feel like I'm a prisoner in solitary confinement, no one to talk to and nowhere to run.

I keep having the same nightmare over and over every night. There's screaming and glass bottles broken on the kitchen floor. He's holding the gun, pointing it straight at me. Tears run down my face as he pulls the trigger and I abruptly wake up. Cold sweats, sheets soaked. I can't stop the tears as I shake in fear through the night. Four nights of that so far. I'm terrified to close my eyes and let my dreams take over. I have no control over my mind when I'm awake and now I have lost control over it when I'm asleep too. I just want this to end.

I think of ways to end my life at least five times every day. Brainstorming ideas for when I get out of here and get my parents off my back. Gun. Pills. Inhalation.

In college, I got tired of painkillers and started inhaling the things that bakeries use to create whipped cream. Weird, I know, but it was an easily accessible and cheap fad. A lot of alcohol and a few inhales would lead to a short high, numbing my mind and making me forget all my problems. It's ironic how I always frowned upon "druggies" growing up and now I had become one in an odd, twisted way.

This disease has changed me. Created fear from doubt and sadness from joy. No matter what I do, where I go, or who I am with it follows me and pulls me back into the abyss. Don't get me wrong. I have "good" days, weeks, and sometimes even a month if I'm lucky. But the moment I feel that pull on my mind is the moment I lose control. The worst is when it happens in a public place like work. I feel the negativity slowly consume my thoughts and it takes everything in me to get through the day.

When he left me, I cried for hours until hours turned into nights and days. I cried driving to work, lost in my own thoughts during the long commute. I tried to hide the pain, but they knew. I didn't want to let anyone in because I didn't want them to know what I was feeling or thinking. I just wanted to get through another day.

Run, pray, cry, drink, repeat. The same routine day in and day out until I couldn't run any longer and the prayers began to shorten. I had reached the edge and there was no turning back. While the edge seems scary, there is also a feeling of liberation. So close to ending it all and never having to feel the pain again.

I'm so mad I couldn't do it – end it. It makes me hate myself even more. Will I ever be able to? Or will I live with this demon my whole life?

Vanessa started going to Bible studies with other individuals in the hospital. They only meet twice a week, but I think it will be a good way to uplift her broken spirit. Her father told me she grew up in the church and was always very active in small groups and mission trips. He said he wasn't very religious, but faith was something important to Vanessa.

I spoke to Vanessa regarding her faith, but her thoughts seemed far beyond confused. She isn't quite sure what she believes in anymore (even though I've noticed her Bible on the nightstand). Her father dropped off her Bible, along with some other books, and a few journaling items. I've noticed her open it here and there, but she seems to focus more on journaling and reading another book in her free time.

Hopefully, we can get her involved in a church community following her release. Although she's lived here for almost a year now, she still hasn't found a church family. It sounds like her and her ex never committed to finding a steady church due to his profession and the lack of free time on Sundays. However, she did tell me that they would read scripture and devotions together, but they often became distracted when life got busy. I wonder if she noticed those subtle changes in her commitment to her faith when she became so committed to him.

Nineteen one four three. Psalms 143. I've read this chapter over and over again for the past couple of weeks (before I was ever admitted here), but now it seems even more relevant being stuck in here. David is praying for "deliverance from his enemies" and I relate to his feeling of hopelessness, despair, and sadness.

[3]"For the enemy has pursued me, crushing my life to the ground, making me sit in darkness like those long dead. [4]Therefore my spirit faints within me; my heart within me is appalled."

How could my God let someone feel this way? How could he let me feel this way? I long for the answers and, until I get them, I cannot accept that he exists. If he existed, then my "man of God" ex-boyfriend would not have betrayed me like this. If he existed, then he would never let me feel this way day in and day out. What kind of God places thoughts of suicide in his own creation's mind?

I have struggled with this question since I first started dealing with depression. If God never gives us anything we can't handle then why is he allowing me to be crushed? When I was younger it was much easier to just "have faith" and believe that God will give me strength. I no longer have that faith.

I want to, I really do, but I literally cannot wrap my mind around the concept of faith anymore. My brain cannot fathom blind faith and that's scary. My beliefs were always the one thing that kept me from carrying out my suicidal thoughts. But now that I have no beliefs, what will stop me?

If life has no purpose then why the fuck am I here? I've heard that suicide is an unforgivable sin so it always scared me out of following through with it. I wanted to go to heaven, but if there is no heaven then what am I waiting for? Depression is the enemy and the break-up itself was tough, but the loss of my faith was my ultimate downfall. The moment I stopped believing in God was the moment I decided to stop fighting. The enemy had won.

Sure, I had plenty of reasons to live such as my family and friends, but what good was I to them if I kept dragging them down? I didn't want to lean on them, but I could no longer lean on God either. This thought process is what led me to believe that there was only one option left: suicide.

Which, speaking of, was still on my mind. Every day I've been in here the thoughts haven't gone away. My mind is swimming in dark blue and all the ideas of how to stop the pain and end my life. I wish my medications could make them stop, but there is no easy fix. If there was an easy fix then I guess I wouldn't be here in the first place.

Kayleigh

Ten years ago I was very much like Vanessa – beaten down, broken, and ready to give up. My mixed emotions and depressing thoughts landed me in the same exact hospital she is currently admitted at. That was the last time I was at this hospital - when I was released ten years ago. I haven't told her this, nor have I told any of my new friends since I moved back to this city.

It took me over a year to heal from the traumatizing experience, but I still wouldn't say I'm fully recovered. Everyone told me that it would get easier, but for weeks it just seemed to get harder and harder. Every day became blurrier and every night grew longer. I couldn't eat or sleep and I refused to get out of bed. No one told me it would be easy, but I didn't think it would be that hard. Moving back home and being isolated gave me a greater sense of failure and hopelessness.

I would lay in my bed with my headphones on, listening to music as my thoughts drifted off to a foggy place. Since I was struggling with my beliefs (as I'm sure Vanessa is right now) music was my saving grace. It numbed my mind temporarily and allowed me to escape the black hole of my reality.

I wish I could tell Vanessa all of this, but I'm pretty sure she wouldn't believe me if I did.

He called today. I can't believe he actually returned my call even though our parents advised against it. I'm not sure why I even want to see him, but I feel like I need closure if that's even possible. I want things to end on a good note before he leaves Arizona.

He told me he is going back home to the east coast for the off-season and won't be at our house when I get released from here. I was crushed to learn this, but what did I expect? We tried living together following the split, but it was too stressful for each of us. Although he broke my heart he still tried his hardest to help me figure things out post break-up.

Before I discovered all of the lies it just seemed like another break-up. While it was painful, it was also civil. There were copious hours of crying on either ends, but never disrespect or hateful words – just sadness. We tried to respect each other throughout the process and worked through details of living arrangements and our dog. How badly I wish we could get back to that... before everything got messy.

When they say a woman's intuition is never wrong, they were right. Although he kept telling me there was no other explanation for the break-up (besides the fact he fell "out of love" with me), I had this terrible feeling in the pit of my stomach. He had never lied to me though so I had no reason to think that he was lying. The thought never crossed my mind that there could have been something, or someone, else.

Eventually, I started receiving anonymous messages that implied that my ex had been talking to another woman. This was only a week after the split so I confronted him only to hear him tell me that he would never do such a thing. His word was enough for me to stop prying for the meantime, but things still didn't make sense. It felt like there was a missing puzzle piece and I couldn't quite solve it. He left for a week to see family and ended up visiting a completely different state. I was uneasy about his abrupt change in plans and why he hadn't told me. I wanted the truth, and if he wasn't going to give it to me then I would find it myself.

First, I found the email receipt for the Valentine's Day flowers and gifts sent to her home in a completely different state (only 2 weeks following our split). Then it was the emails full of plane ticket itineraries flying her out west for big events with his agency. I was in shock. If he was willing to show her off this quickly following our long relationship, then how long had this been going on for?

The next 6 hours were a blur. Following my shocking discovery, I experienced every type of negative emotion you could think of: confusion, sadness, anger, rage. I reached a level of rage that I had never encountered before that day. Confronting him and hearing him tell me that it had been going on for a long time broke me. No, it destroyed me. How could I be so dumb? So clueless? What was real and what was a lie? Was anything he ever told me real? Like when we talked about marriage and jokingly talked about names for our children one day. My reality was shattered.

I left work in a hurry that day, recklessly driving home to find my gun. I remember throwing a wine bottle at the floor and screaming in frustration as I struggled to find the gun that my ex so carefully hid. I was home alone, but I knew that he was going to come home to try and calm me down.

Then, next thing I know, the cops are in my apartment, handcuffing me for being an endangerment to myself.

"Vanessa, I didn't know what to do. I'm worried. Please just let them help you. I'm scared."

I know he was just trying to help, but was this the answer? The cops then gave me two options: jail or the mental hospital. Apparently throwing a wine bottle at the floor when you're home alone is considered domestic violence. As stupid as it sounds, I told them to take me to jail because at least then I would have rights and the possibility of getting out sooner. Well, it turns out I already had no rights because my ex signed a petition for the cops to take me into the UPC (aka the looney-fucking-bin).

Imagine sitting in your own home, depressed and mentally fucked up. Then imagine that with the addition of handcuffs that are cutting into your wrists for over an hour while you wait for paperwork to be filled out and another car to arrive. I was no longer a human being. I was an object to them. A victim in the mental health system.

The worst part was having to call my boss from the UPC and tell him what was going on. You don't really know humility until you have to tell your boss that you won't be at work (for God knows how long) because your ex-boyfriend had admitted you into the looney bin. How fucking embarrassing. I'm not sure if God feels like my life is a joke, but it sure as hell feels like it.

Kayleigh

The day I got released from the hospital so many years ago is still crystal clear in my mind today (which is actually quite surprising considering how drunk I was the remainder of the day). The moment I left the hospital I went straight to the liquor store. For the next 48 hours straight, I pumped copious amounts of alcohol into my system. Anything that would make me feel numb and ease the pain.

The side effects consisted of racing thoughts, inability to sleep, and repetitive vomiting. I didn't care though, as long as the numbness continued. I felt like my life was over and I was tired of following the rules. Similar to Vanessa, I was embarrassed by my situation so instead of getting back to reality, I ignored it.

These are the very reasons I am scared to release Vanessa too early. While she probably feels like she's at rock bottom right now, the worst is yet to come. The next few weeks following her release will determine her outcome: recovery or relapse.

Therefore, my biggest priority right now is making sure Vanessa has a stable and safe environment to go home to. Her parents have decided that it would be best for her to move back in with them on the east coast. She will have to leave her job here, but at least she will be surrounded with a strong support system back home. She's having a hard time accepting this decision right now, but she will see it's in her best interest down the road.

They think that moving back home will be the best thing for me. What do they even know? I lost my voice in here and now it looks like I've lost it out there too. Powerless. 23 years old and I seem to have lost all control of my life. But I can't fight it... agreeing to this move is my ticket out of here. If I don't comply, then they will bring me back in.

I know my family thinks moving back home is the best option, but what about my life here? I will be letting so many people down by leaving. It breaks my heart thinking about leaving my student-athletes at the high school. They need me. And quite frankly, I need them too. It's hard to explain the feeling I get from my profession. It's definitely a love-hate relationship, but mostly love. It gives me purpose and brings me so much joy. Like when an athlete comes up to me at the end of the season to thank me for getting them healthy, or for helping them during what seems like the hardest time of their lives. Most of them are so appreciative and it feels good to know I can make a difference in these young peoples' minds.

The athletic director told the students and coaches that I went on vacation, but they all know I would never leave them so abruptly for something like that. Just thinking about it is stressing me out, and now that I have to resign and move, all that stress is building up. How will I tell them? What will I tell them?

I hate that I'm being forced to run away from my life here instead of facing it head on. I think that this is a huge mistake and I'm already dreading this move. Plus, I feel isolated from most of my friends and family anyway. I know that they care, but by the time they realized how badly I needed help it was too late. I know

I'll get over it, but they're really the last people I want to be around right now. Except my youngest brother. He always knows the right thing to say and somehow understands me when I'm feeling low. But I don't want him to see me like this. I really don't want anyone to see me like this.

Being back in this place has brought my mind back to some of my darkest memories. No matter how long it's been, the memories never fade. Unfortunately, I cannot forget what happened that year. This experience has been challenging for me because it is the first time I've had to face my demons.

Maybe taking Vanessa's case was meant to be. I'm a firm believer that everything happens for a reason so there has to be a reason God led me back here. I need to be strong for Vanessa so I can help her get through what I once went through. If I would've had someone to guide me when I was in her position then the process might have gone a little smoother.

My struggles in the past brought me to where I am today and compelled me to help others through my career. The lack of understanding and education regarding mental health in this country is appalling. Although I'm only a small piece in a bigger picture, I believe I can make a difference. The stigmas society places on individuals with mental health conditions is enough to push them to the edge. In order to help the patients I work with I also need to impact the world around me. Only then will we see a positive change in our mental health system.

Vanessa

A new girl got admitted last night. There's about twenty women in my wing, but I haven't really connected with any of them. Most of them have serious drug issues with Xanax, heroine, or meth. One woman is detoxing from meth and it's really scary. She says that she sees people that aren't here and hears random voices and noises. Part of her face is scarred because she used to scratch herself when she was hallucinating. It's crazy because she is such a nice lady, but you can tell she is lost. I thought my personal battle was hard, but she's got it bad.

The new girl looks like she's around my age, maybe even younger. She got admitted after we all went to bed, but I heard her getting checked in when I got up for the bathroom. I introduced myself to her this morning and I'm glad I did because we actually have a lot in common. Leah is currently a college student and a couple years younger than me. She landed herself in here after an overdose of anxiety medication. She's a nursing student and told me she was just really stressed out from school and felt like she experienced a small moment of weakness. Her dad is working on getting her out of here as soon as possible. I think they might even get a lawyer involved since they won't release her yet. It's nice to have a friend in here, even if it is just for a little while. It makes the days a little more bearable.

One thing that is not bearable is my roommate's snoring at night. She snores so loud I can hear it through my ear plugs. Therefore, I get ZERO sleep. They keep telling me that they will move me to another room, but no luck so far. Despite her snoring though, my roommate isn't so bad. She was diagnosed with manic depression at a young age and has been dealing with it for decades.

That blows my mind. DECADES. I can't imagine dealing with this disease for decades. I'm pretty sure she voluntarily checked in here, but she is starting to get antsy. They've held her here for 28 days... that's wild. However, her long stay here has allowed her to learn the ropes in this hospital. For example, she taught me how to hide forbidden items in our room like pens, food, shower items, etc. While her mind is a bit scattered, I'm thankful for her guidance here. It's interesting to see how certain circumstances can bring the oddest people together.

Kayleigh

Walking out of my therapy session today I can't stop thinking about Vanessa. I've been keeping up with my therapy appointments ever since I moved back to Arizona. I haven't done them consistently over the past 10 years, but sometimes I just need that extra support. One thing I have consistently used over the years to help manage my depression is medication. Anti-depressants daily and anti-anxiety medicine as needed. It's not easy to rely on drugs, but it really does help sometimes.

The topic of medications is always a tough one because some patients rely on them while others want nothing to do with them. I, personally, was against it for the longest time until I found the right combination for me. They are more of a precaution than anything. They helped "balance" me when I felt like I might lose control. The anxiety medicine is used less often. It is great for when I am feeling anxious or get stressed, but it also makes me feel fuzzy or tired so I try not to use it unless absolutely needed. That's the bad thing about medications... they can change you. Sometimes it's hard to face the fact that I need a little extra help now and then.

I'm not sure what route Vanessa will take, but I hope she at least considers using some medications. Even if it is just temporary, I think that it will help keep her steady through the rough patch over these next few months.

Vanessa

I'm furious. Leah just got here and they've already given her an early release date. I guess her dad threatened to sue the hospital for holding her against their will. I mean, I'm happy for her, but I'm pissed I couldn't get a release date that fast. And, I know this sounds selfish, but I don't want her to leave yet... our friendship has helped me stay positive these past 24 hours and I'm scared to deal with this place alone again.

Another new girl arrived last night. I honestly haven't seen anyone come in here looking as sad and lost as her. She didn't say one word when she got in and went straight to her room. Leah and I decided we needed to make her feel comfortable so we invited her to breakfast with us.

Marie is a 21 year old single mother of two children – one son and one daughter. 24 hours ago she decided to stab herself in the abdomen because she couldn't handle life anymore. Her husband is apparently a jackass and leaves her and the children on a weekly basis. She is from a small town out in western Arizona and works as a manager at a restaurant to support her family. There isn't a lot of opportunity where she's from and felt like she had run out of options.

Marie has to meet with the doctors more than Leah and I because her stab wound is infected. On top of that, she just found out she is pregnant with her third child. Maybe that has something to do with why she stabbed herself in the stomach... I'm not sure if she knew about this pregnancy before or after she decided to end her life. I didn't want to ask because I don't think it's appropriate right now. I can't even imagine what she is dealing with, but I really want to help her get through this.

We finally got her to try and eat something, but between her wound and the pregnancy she could barely hold anything down. Except cheeseburgers. That's pretty much all we will eat because everything else is disgusting.

In other news, I've been using the phone a lot during our free time (which is a lot). I've been talking to my family and friends, but mostly just one friend – Rob. Before I was admitted here Rob and I had been messaging here and there regarding faith and my recent struggles with it. He had seen some of my social media posts and decided to reach out to me and check in. It was so kind of him to do that and continue to encourage me while I'm in here. It just seems so natural talking to him about all of this because he knows the right thing to say. I'm hoping his strong faith can help me find mine again.

A few people I wish I could speak to more are my siblings. It's a tough situation because my brothers are younger so it's not their place to be strong for me. It would be nice to hear their comforting voices more often, but what I miss the most right now is my big sister.

When I was younger I remember sitting in my sister's room with her whenever she was sad or upset. I never really understood what was going on, but I liked knowing we could sit there together without saying a word and just know that we were there for one another. I always felt lucky to have an older sister to look up to and lean on. But, right now, we were further apart than ever. She was scared and angry when I told her I was suicidal. I don't blame her. I guess I would be angry too, but I need her. I wish she knew how sorry I was, but I would give anything to hear some of her sarcastic jokes right now.

My mom calls every day. You'd think we would run out of things to talk about, but she does a good job of distracting me from my situation. She usually just updates me on her day or my brothers' sporting events or activities. Nothing exciting, but it takes my mind away from the sadness for a few short moments. She's probably worried sick, but she has done one hell of job staying strong for me.

My family may be different from me, but I think they are learning how to understand me more and more with each day. I know they will never fully understand, but I also know they love me, and that's enough for right now.

Kayleigh

"MENTAL STATUS EXAM:

Identification: Actual age is 23, apparent age as stated. Appearance: She is of medium height, medium build, clean, neat, currently wearing casual clothing. Behaviors: Normal sensorium, normal posture, good eye contact, normal motor level, and satisfactory attention span. No mannerisms. Personality traits: She is currently open, gender appropriate, actively cooperative. Style is worried. Affect is inappropriate to content. Intermittently, the patient is smiling and laughing when discussing severity of concerns regarding gun situation. Subjective mood is depressed. Objective mood is anxious. Thought content: No delusions or illusions. She acknowledges suicidal ideations with a plan to shoot herself. She denies thoughts of harming others. Cognition: She is alert and oriented. Judgement is impaired. Insight is fair. Her risk is high to medium."

Vanessa's mental status exam report from the Urgent Psychiatric Care center was sent to me shortly after she arrived at the hospital. From what I read, it sounds like she held herself together well considering the circumstances. However, there are still things that I need to address with her before she is released. My biggest concern is that she was reacting with smiles and laughs when the UPC social worker discussed the severity of the situation with her. I've been trying to get Vanessa to open up regarding her stay at the UPC, but she keeps blowing it off. It's like she has shut off all communication regarding those 24 hours, but I can't help her if she won't open up. I know it's difficult, but she needs to try.

Vanessa

It's dark and I can barely see anything. There are people screaming obscenities and others crying. The girl next to me is curled up in a ball in her chair, sobbing because the man in front of her is mocking her while trying to force her to take medication. When the girl looks up, I realize the girl is me.

Another nightmare. Add it to the list of ones I already have every night. So, I apologize when Kayleigh asks me to relive my experience at the Urgent Psychiatric Care center and I refuse. It's a terrifying thing to be scared of your own memories. You can't erase them, no matter how hard you try.

Nor can I erase this feeling of deep sadness. Every night I fall into a deeper shade of dark blue. During the day, I sometimes feel like I have it under control, but then the sadness swallows me when night falls. I wish I felt numb because numbness would be better than feeling pain. I would choose to be emotionless forever if it meant escaping this feeling.

Depression is such an ugly thing. People talk about, doctors "treat" it, and everyone else tries to help you cope with it. But no one ever really knows what it's like until they experience it firsthand. Always stuck in this constant cycle of asking for help, and then wanting to be alone and avoid the world. I feel as if there is no end to this vicious cycle – except to end it myself.

Why do I feel this way and no one else does? All of my friends and family are normal... and then there's me. I have so much going for me so why do I feel like a weight is holding me down, dragging me to the darkest depths of my own thoughts? I need a way out. I am praying for a way out.

Kayleigh

Vanessa has told me how difficult it is for her to open up about her experience at the UPC. She told the doctor that she constantly has nightmares from that night. Unfortunately, I don't think those demons will stop haunting her for a while.

I remember my personal experience at the UPC, as much as I try to forget it. It was appalling. I don't know any other way to describe it. There are people there that are mentally unstable in a dangerous way. And I'm not talking about self harm or suicide, I'm talking about people that could potentially go ape shit crazy and lash out against the people around them.

Just imagine – 40 mentally unstable men and women all stuck in close quarters in one small room. You are in arm's reach of each individual to your right and left. When I was there, they had some magazines and books to read while you were in there. Vanessa said they got rid of the Bible they used to have because people were practicing odd religious acts that were disrupting the atmosphere. She said reading the Bible was something that calmed her and without access to that at the UPC she became even more anxious and scared.

I know she is reliving her UPC experience in her nightmares, but I hope she can open up to the doctor or myself soon. The sooner she can open up, the sooner she can face her fears, and the sooner she can start to heal.

Vanessa

Out of all the negative things I could say about my experience in the mental health system thus far, my biggest disappointment has been the way I've been treated by the employees. You would think that all of the nurses, doctors, and therapists would be kind and warm, but instead they have been nothing but rude and cold.

I will especially never forget the male nurse at the UPC who was rude to me. He continually laughed at the fact that a "girl like me" would be suicidal and end up in a place like this. He repeatedly ignored my requests to update me on my care and told me that my life should be perfect and I had no reason to be suicidal. Did he take a simple moment to ask why I was suicidal or what was causing me to feel that way? No. He did not ask one question of concern or even show one ounce of respect while demeaning me and my situation. The only word I can use to describe his treatment toward me was dehumanizing. He looked at me and spoke to me like an animal. No, not even an animal – an object.

It's like the workers at the UPC just pretended we didn't exist. The only help they offered was to shoot up a patient with sleeping medications or to help strap them down if they were getting out of control. As I observed their behavior for the next 24 hours, I was appalled. It was sickening to see the patients treated in such a crude manner.

It really makes me wonder if that place has ever been sued. I've been writing everything down that has been inappropriate between the UPC and here. At first I did it out of anger, but now I'm truly concerned this is an issue nationwide within our mental health system. If I don't help change it, then who will?

For example, is it legal for my psychiatrist to tell me "If I do not take my medications, then I will not be released as fast?" Considering I have been 100 percent cooperative and active in "therapy" groups, I'm not sure the best option is to threaten me. Once again, I feel like I have no control over anything.

I haven't seen many movies regarding mental health hospitals, but from what I have seen prior to this experience, I thought I would have more rights than I do now. Like my right to be treated like a fucking human being. But, hey, I guess that idea got lost in translation when our mental health system started to care more about profit than people.

Kayleigh

I will be the first to admit that I have been lazy. I, like Vanessa, had so many complaints about our mental health system, but what have I really done to change that? Sure, I became a social worker, but this young girl sits in front of me suffering from the same fucked up system I was once lost in.

She is struggling today. I can see it in her face – glossy eyes, red from tears. The worry in her mind shows in the wrinkles on her forehead while the bags under her eyes show sleeplessness. No smile from her today, not even a forced one. She is quiet and that scares me.

Quietness means that her mind is probably racing with thoughts. The moment we hit silence our minds start to suffocate us with memories, feelings, and intense emotions. This is the moment depression grabs ahold of you. It catches you in your one moment of weakness, latches on, and holds tight for as long as your mind allows it to.

This was the biggest challenge for me when I was younger – learning to nip the darkness in the butt before it latched on. For months, I would hit a wall every night and have to fight that moment. Some nights (most nights) I didn't fight hard enough. It was just easier to accept defeat sometimes. When you have been fighting the same battle every day, you can't expect to win every time.

Well, it may have taken me many years to learn, but I figured out I could fight that daily battle and win (almost every time). While mental health disorders are based off of chemical imbalances in the brain, another large part of the puzzle is "mind over matter." My concept of mind of matter was built on my foundation with Christ. I know that I am strong in my weaknesses and, with Christ, I will win every time. Now, the question is, how do I get Vanessa there? It's out of my scope to discuss religion with her, but there has to be a way for me to guide her in the right direction with therapy and group sessions following her release. It's worth a shot at least.

Leah got released yesterday and I am feeling more alone than ever. Marie is still here, but she has also been really sick from her wound healing. Leah helped take my mind off of all this shit because we would always be making fun and laughing at stupid jokes together. Now that she's gone I feel just as lonely as I did when I first got here. I know I only have a couple more days, but every hour feels like eternity in here.

My life feels like one of those movies where the main character relives the same day over and over again. Wake up. Breakfast. Meds. Group session. Lunch. Free time. Group session. Visitation. Dinner. Meds. Sleep. Repeat. The 10 minute elliptical sessions during recreation group time aren't cutting it anymore. I can't even keep track of how many stupid drawings I have colored since I've been here. I definitely can't imagine making another dumbass bracelet or coloring another mandala worksheet for the rest of my life. Not only do they treat us like children, but now we are "getting the privilege" to do activities like them too. Fucking spare me.

You're telling me this is the "best" private mental hospital in the entire state of Arizona and this is the best we can do? Fucking bead bracelets, coloring books, and board games? Dear God, I hope not. I can't even imagine what the other, less privileged hospitals offer.

I'm still baffled at the fact there isn't mandatory outdoor activities or more time to access exercise equipment. I have been outside once my entire time here for a group sing-along activity. The only other time to go outside is for smoke breaks, and I hate being around smoke so I can't go outside then. Don't these idiots know that a little bit of Vitamin D and a lot of physical activity can go a long way? But then again, what do they really know? Not much apparently.

This hospital environment continues to trigger some heavy emotions for me. Last night, I lost it. For some reason I allowed the emotions to overcome me and, for the first time in a long time, I cried. I cried until there was nothing left. The worst part is that I have no idea why I was even feeling that way. Why does this disease attack at the most random times?

This just goes to show how hard it can be dealing with depression. I've had time to learn how to stop it from escalating, but that doesn't mean it will completely go away. I wish it were that easy for my sake and Vanessa's. What I struggle with the most is how my faith isn't strong enough to overcome this once and for all. Is the enemy working to break me down individually or is everyone dealing with mental illnesses really this screwed? If my God is so great, then why would He allow the enemy to pursue me despite my devotion and persistence? Sometimes I start to think that it's my fault for feeling this way and I forget that there is something (or someone) bigger working against me and God's will.

This is the issue Vanessa is struggling with right now. She keeps asking why God made her this way and why He would allow the enemy to pursue her so ferociously. I wish I could guide her, but I'm not sure I even know the answer to her questions. I'm still trying to figure it out on my own.

One of my coworkers was talking about his faith to nonbelievers the other day. He made a statement along the lines of "God allows bad things to happen to us for lessons and greater purpose unbeknownst to us." While I support this idea in some cases, I just can't apply that to cases of depression and suicide. Yes, I am now trying to help others because of the darkness I escaped, but I wouldn't wish that on anyone just for a "bigger purpose" of creating a platform to help others. I would rather help others without having to go through so many bad episodes that almost killed me. While my faith is strong, I still have so many questions that need answered.

Vanessa

Remember when your parents finally decided to tell you that Santa Claus wasn't real? Even though you wanted so hard to believe in him again, you just couldn't. That's the equivalent to how I feel about God right now. I want to believe, I do, but I just can't. It's like there is a black pit in my heart and soul where my love for Christ once resided. This feeling is new to me. Terrifying. Even more so than depression itself.

How do I find my faith again? Will it come back to me like a once forgotten memory, or is it lost forever? I'm not sure who to talk to about this. I've tried prayer journaling like I used to, but it seems forced and fake. I used to feel like my prayers were heard, but now I feel like my words echo into nothingness.

I have attended the "church" service or Bible studies they offer here, but all I feel is frustration and isolation. How can I feel so lonely in an environment I once felt accepted? I am searching, seeking, calling out for Christ and all I hear are the sound of crickets. No response. No reciprocation. WHERE IS MY GOD? He isn't here, I can tell you that much. If good and evil do exist, then the enemy is more present in my life than Christ right now.

If I make it out of this alive I'm not sure I'll call myself a Christian anymore. How could I when my God let me fall when He was supposed to catch me? My unfailing God has failed me and I'm not sure I need any more disappointments in my life right now.

Kayleigh

Tomorrow is Vanessa's release day. I'm not sure if I'm more excited or worried for her. Do I think she's ready to get back to the real world? No. But I also don't think staying in this place will fix her problems either. Her father had to fly back to the east coast so he gave her two best friends permission to pick her up when she is released.

Her friends have already started packing up her belongings from the house she shared with her ex-boyfriend. The least amount of time she has to spend in that house the better off she will be. I'm sure almost every room in that house will be a trigger for her, especially her bedroom.

Vanessa recently opened up to me about one of the nights she was home alone and sat in her bedroom contemplating suicide. She had bought the gun weeks ago, but still hadn't shot it yet. She had the gun in her hand and kept putting up it to her head. She would get scared, set the gun back down, and then repeat that over and over again, contemplating ending it all. Vanessa told me that she barely ever shot guns before, let alone a revolver. She wasn't even sure if she would do it the right way. So, to practice, she shot the gun randomly at the bedroom closet wall.

She remembers her dog leaving her side and running into the other room, scared from the loud noise. Tears started to flow down her face and she knew that she needed to ask for help. She knew that her suicidal thoughts were escalating quickly and this just put her one step closer to ending it all. With that being said, I would imagine seeing that hole in the wall or sleeping in her bedroom will be difficult for her. While I want her to be comfortable in her own bed, I also don't want her to be surrounded by negative memories.

I'm hoping the presence of her friends will help her get by until she moves out later this week.

Vanessa

Today is THE day. The day I escape this prison they call an "oasis." Jay and Al will be here at noon to sign the paperwork and pick me up. This is the first time in weeks I have felt any sense of hope. Finally, something to look forward to. No more cafeteria food. No more mandatory meds. No more sleep disruptions throughout the night. No. More. Bullshit.

They even said that they would bring my dog so I can see her first thing! I can't wait for her to jump out of the car and into my arms. I don't care what people say – dogs are one of the most therapeutic things on this planet.

Once they pick me up the plan is to continue the packing they started and finish planning the long road trip home. Al has to fly back tomorrow, but Jay is going to help me drive across the country. We are planning to stop at my sister's in the Midwest at some point. My family thinks it'll be good for me to see my nieces and nephew, but I'm honestly really nervous. They make me happier than anything on this earth, but I'm scared for them to see me this way. I don't know if I can pretend to be happy in front of them. They know me as a fun, loving auntie, but I look in the mirror and see everything but that.

I also finished a book today called Unbroken. My dad dropped it off at the beginning of my stay here. I'm not sure if he knew the storyline, but wow, he couldn't have picked a better book for me to read during this experience. The ending showed so much forgiveness and now I feel guilty for holding so much hate in my heart. I want to make a conscious effort to change that, but it's not as easy as it sounds.

One day at a time though, and today is just the beginning of a long journey.

Kayleigh

Vanessa left a couple of hours ago. Now the nervousness sets in for me. An uneasy feeling will linger inside me for the next few days, weeks, and sometimes even months. Another patient released, another waiting game. You really never know what is going to happen next... Will she end up being okay? Will she end up back in a mental health institution? Or worse, will she end up dead? These are serious thoughts that cross my mind every time a patient is released.

She was the happiest I've seen her all week today. You should've seen her when her dog ran up to her outside of the hospital. Pure joy. I should find a way to get the hospital to allow pet visits when patients are admitted here.

Vanessa's stay here has truly inspired me to create change. I've stood aside too long hoping our mental health system would change, but it's time for me to make that change. I will make it my goal to improve the care that individuals receive in mental health institutions such as this one, and I won't stop until I know things are right.

My job may have been to help Vanessa, but she has helped me more than I could have ever imagined. This case has been a wake-up call for me and it's time for me to stop dreaming. I will create change for myself, for Vanessa, and for those who follow in the future.

PART TWO

When I woke up and got out of bed this morning I wasn't sure if I was going to vomit or fall over first. I felt sick to my stomach, and overly dehydrated to say the least. Was I hungover or still drunk from last night? I'm not quite sure. I about had a heart attack this morning when I woke up and turned over to see a guy in my bed. My friend had stayed the night to make sure I was okay after I had one too many drinks out at the bar. Jay and Al said it would be best for him to stay and watch over me throughout the night.

I don't know if I feel sick from the amount of alcohol I drank or the mixture of medications I forced into my body throughout the past 24 hours. Anti-depressants for the sadness. Anxiety pills for restlessness. Adderall for a little boost to get shit done. I was completely sober when I started taking them earlier in the day and I honestly had no idea I would be drinking later that night. My intention was never to mix medications and alcohol, but once I had one drink I couldn't stop.

After Jay and Al picked me up yesterday, my initial feeling of freedom and excitement immediately dissipated the moment I walked into my home. It was like every memory that had been consuming my mind the past few weeks flooded through me all at once. I felt sadness, anger, confusion, fear. The overwhelming feeling of loneliness, even though I wasn't truly alone. My boyfriend and I hadn't even lived in our new house together, yet it felt like every memory we shared resided within those walls. The hole in the closet wall was still there as a reminder of my stupidity one of those dreadful nights. Everything was just how I left it, but at the same time nothing felt the same. I still hadn't come to terms with moving across the country and leaving everything behind. I had come to love this home, my job, and my life here. But now, I wondered if I really ever loved it or if I just loved the idea of it.

After the initial shock wore off, I felt a brief sense of calm knowing that my two best friends were here to help me fill the void. On top of them being here, a lot of my other friends and family stopped by to check in, help pack, and say goodbyes.

My heart was constantly racing throughout the day once all the medications started kicking in. I felt a little less foggy from a depression standpoint, but the anxiety pills were making me feel a bit fuzzy. It felt like my thoughts were moving too fast for me to even think... if that even makes sense.

The guys filled me in on last night's festivities (hence the head-pounding hangover) and this is apparently where I made some not-so-bright decisions. They didn't know that I had been taking all of those pills, but I did, and I still decided to drink beyond a level of drunkenness. Despite the poor decisions and hangover, I would do it all over again. Last night was the first time I've had fun in a long time. I felt "happy" (even if it was due to a little help from the copious amounts of substances I consumed). I finally felt alive, even if just for one night.

Back to reality though. I had to pick up some items from the high school and say my goodbyes today. Leaving the school left me with an empty feeling inside, like I had lost a piece of me. I chose my career path because I love what I do – helping others, being active, making positive impacts on young minds. My job is not a job to me. It's a passion – something that allows me to pour myself into others and, in return, brings me purpose.

I've never been jobless until now. I started working as a young teenager and I can honestly say there has never been a day in my life I haven't worked – until now. 23 years old, one year out of college, and I'm already unemployed and moving back in with my parents. Talk about failure. I have never known failure to this extent before and I can personally say it feels pretty shitty. All I've ever wanted to do was make my parents proud, and having a job was one way for me to do that. I never wanted my brothers to see their big sister fail either. The pressure of being a role model felt like the entire world was on my shoulders, crushing me. What would they think now, seeing their big sister mess up and start from scratch?

Some of the athletes I built relationships with came in to say goodbye today. I tried my hardest not to get emotional, but I couldn't help but let a few tears surface. How do you say goodbye to individuals who had such a profound impact on your life? I've lost a lot of relationships throughout this experience, so saying goodbye to more wasn't easy. These kids have taught me more than I would have ever imagined. They gave me hope on my lowest days without even knowing how much they truly impacted me.

I have one student who helps with athletic training duties on a daily basis. She is someone that I have spent the most time with during my days at the high school. Mentoring her has been a blessing in itself. Except, right now, I feel like I am letting her down by leaving. I know that she understands, but I feel terrible. Watching her grow as an athletic training student and young adult has been an honor, but now I can't help but wonder if she will still look up to me once I'm gone.

A handful of people actually know what happened these past few weeks. One of them was a student I had been working with from the beginning of the year. He had opened up to me in the past about some personal things he dealt with – one being that his father committed suicide when he was younger. He was always attentive and I think his past helped him to form an idea that I was struggling recently. Although I least expected it from one of my student-athletes, he actually brought me a lot of hope and positivity during those dark days. I wish I could tell him and the other students how much they truly helped me.

Driving home from the high school, I couldn't help but to reminisce about all the memories I had there. My first real job. Friendships. Mentorships. New experiences, both good and bad. I knew that I would especially miss my supervisor at the high school and a fellow colleague from the clinic I was contracted through. They were both so kind throughout this whole experience and never once were they judgmental. Without their support, this transition could have been a lot worse. Somewhere in all this sadness of leaving though something made me feel like this could be for the best. How could I help others if I didn't help myself first?

When I got home I went straight back into the same bad habits. Take some pills, drink some booze, pack some shit, repeat. I stopped keeping track of when I had taken my medications because 1) I don't care and 2) even if I did, I truly couldn't remember. Everything was crazy, but calm at the same time. I don't know how to describe it, but I liked it a lot better than the place my mind wandered to.

The drugs aren't enough to drown it out completely though. Suicide is always on my mind. Even when I'm not consciously thinking of it, my subconscious is hoarding those dark thoughts until it's time for them to resurface. Every morning I wake up suicide is the first thing on my mind and every night my head hits that pillow the suicidal thoughts flood my mind once again. There's no escaping a darkness when you can't even get one light to turn on.

I've had some pretty long spouts of suicidal thoughts before, but never this long. Every day for the past 6 weeks it has been on my mind, haunting me. I've never experienced them this consistently and that scares me. Terrifies me. Makes me nervous for the future. The persisting dark thoughts have made a permanent residence in my head. The biggest issue now is that, unlike before, I feel like I can't express these feelings to anyone else. The last thing I want is to end up back in an institution. I can't pretend to be happy, but I think that I'll keep these thoughts to myself for as long as I can.

On a lighter note, the guys and I got a bit creative and pulled some harmless pranks on my ex without him knowing it quite yet. The guys thought of this great idea to remove every single lightbulb from the house. Talk about an inconvenience. I am laughing just thinking about the look on my ex's face when he walks back into the house. I feel a little bad, but I guess I could have done a lot worse... although I did do something idiotic last night. I would like to blame my poor decisions on my absolute state of drunkenness, but for some reason I thought it was a good idea to carve the words "F YOU" on one of the kitchen walls. Everyone tried to stop me, but I wasn't having it. I kind of regret that one.

I can't believe I finally leave tomorrow. It feels like just yesterday I moved across the country to embark on this new journey with him. Now, I'm about to leave and he's not even a part of my life anymore. I haven't heard from him since he called while I was in the hospital. This is probably due to multiple reasons – our families are against it, as well as his agent. Not to mention he probably 1) hates me and 2) is terrified of me. Which he has every right to be. My crazy scares me too.

I really fucked up. The night I found out that he cheated I said some pretty messed up things, some pretty scary things. I can honestly say, more than anything, I regret saying those negative things to him. I would like to think he knew I didn't mean any of it, but I'm sure he's questioning my sanity at this point. For some reason, I feel like I'm the one who deserves to be hated even though a lot of this was triggered by his dumb actions. That's the thing about depression though – you search for reasons why you are the one in the wrong and why no one should love you. Why would anyone love me after all the crazy shit I said and did to myself? I can't even love myself.

Some more people stopped by the house to help finish packing and wish me well. I honestly don't remember most of the day though because I'm too focused on trying not to throw up. My body is rejecting all of the toxins I'm putting into it. I weighed myself this morning and I've lost 7 pounds since I was first admitted into the hospital. I guess depression has one positive side effect: weight loss. Don't get me wrong. I love food, but for some reason I can't stomach a damn thing. I am barely ever hungry so even when I try to eat it feels like I'm forcing it. It doesn't help that I haven't been working out either. I know it will help, but I have no energy to do it.

One of the most debilitating things about depression is the effect it has on your body. Yes, it's a mental illness, but it affects everything. You start to sleep less, or maybe even more. The nights I have nightmares lead to little sleep and sluggish days. The nights I sleep way too long turn into sleeping all day and getting absolutely nothing done. My weight is lower than it's ever been because I rarely want to eat. Not to mention, I have this idea that my ex left me because I am not physically attractive enough. I need to lose weight. I need to look a certain way. Maybe if I just look better then I will be happier. Then, there are the days that you just feel so fatigued, so weak. You can't explain it, but you just know it's the depression tugging you back into your bed, closing your blinds and pulling the curtains down. I can feel it in my bones – this disease. Every inch of my body surrenders when it attacks.

In other news, everything is packed and ready to go so I guess I should finally get ready too. Al flew back east today, so it's just Jay and I now. Tomorrow marks the beginning of a new chapter and, whether I like it or not, I need to accept it.

I thought today would be easier considering I would be moving forward and driving away from all the bad memories. Instead, it just gave me a long period of time to sit there and think of every little thing that makes me sad. Jay is a trooper for listening to me sob all damn day. Long story short:

1. The ex-boyfriend posts photo with new girlfriend online.
2. The crazy ex-girlfriend (me) is upset and posts something along the lines of saying how stupid it is to be disrespectful when you still share a house and belongings with him.
3. The ex-boyfriend's mother messages my father threatening to take legal action if I continue to slander her son's name.
4. Father gets pissed at daughter for posting her "feelings" on social media.

Just when I think I have things under control, this shit happens. First and foremost, I couldn't believe that my ex would post something so soon after this mess of an experience. I was shocked. I felt disrespected on a whole new level. Not only had I not heard from him or his mother concerning my well-being, but now I was being legally threated by a woman I once thought cared for me. When did people decide it was okay to not only hurt me, but then to rub it in my face? They had already taken my dignity, my home, my job, and now I could actually really lose EVERYTHING. Also – side note – I'm pretty sure slander consists of false statements. I'm sorry that you think your son is not a lying, cheating asshole, but HELLO, he is. And I know I shouldn't say things like that, but can you blame me? I know better, but I'm angry. Furious. Enraged. Use whatever word you'd like, but I have the right to feel whichever and whatever way I feel about this whole situation right now.

I know I shouldn't make my feelings so public, but I'm so sick of seeing people get away with hurting others. I truly try my best to make decisions that won't hurt others, but when I do make mistakes I apologize. I don't try to cover up my mistakes by attacking someone else. I'm not perfect and I realize that. Therefore, everyone else should start realizing he isn't perfect either. Everyone is so concerned about HIS feelings. HIS reputation. Good to know that I live in a world where a public figure's image takes precedent over treating me like a human being. I feel like I have the firing squad at my back and I have no idea how to respond to this. I'll just keep quiet. Let him be the good guy. Let him have it all. Let him live happily ever after. He deserves it, right?

Despite the amount of disappointment that he and his family have provided me with, one of his family members has continued to check in on me. She doesn't have to, but she does. She chooses to see me for me and not for the mental illnesses that consume my mind. I appreciate that. I appreciate the people who still haven't let me down. It's refreshing to know that I can actually rely on some people (although not many).

Disappointment is a familiar feeling to me these days. Disappointed in myself. Disappointed in others. Mostly disappointed in those closest to me. A lot of people have reached out to me in the past few weeks, but the only people I truly want by my side weren't there when I needed it the most. This was the first time in my life that I felt let down on such a devastating level. When I needed support, no one could be there for me. There was always some excuse – too much work, not enough time, flights are too expensive... the list goes on and on. The only excuse I actually understood was the expense aspect of getting out to the west coast, but even then, my ex had offered to fly anyone and everyone out to be by side when everything went down. So, once again, no excuses.

I'm not trying to sound dramatic, but I honestly feel abandoned by the ones closest to me. Their presence wouldn't have solved the cause of my predicament, but it would have postponed the suicide attempts. Don't they realize that I could be dead right now? I don't think they know how hurt I am. I know I hurt them too by scaring them and now by pushing them away, but those are demons I will have to face when I get home.

I'm too much for friends and family to handle and that makes it impossible for them to help me. Just another reason why I wanted to (and still want to) just finish it already. If I stay, I will just keep hurting the ones I love and dragging them down with me. One painful loss now is nothing compared to a lifetime of annoyance for needing them to support me.

I haven't eaten any real food in two whole days. Well, I have, but I can't keep it down. Maybe it's the two energy drinks I consumed on top of the three Adderall in my system all within 5 hours. Is that enough to give me a heart attack? Because I feel like my heart is going to explode out of my chest right now. I've been throwing up nonstop since we got to my sister's house.

We got to Illinois around dinner time and were greeted by my two beautiful nieces and handsome nephew. I will say there is nothing quite like becoming an aunt. When my first niece was born it was the greatest moment of my life at the time. Even though I didn't have to do any of the hard work (props to you big sister), I felt like I was on top of the world. When I first started dealing with depression, my niece was the main reason I kept fighting. The joy she brought to me and my family gave me hope for brighter days, better days.

I thought that it would be awkward seeing my sister after these past few weeks, but I was wrong. She welcomed me with open arms. We didn't have to say a word in that moment because she knew that I was sorry and I knew that she loved me. We haven't talked about the whole situation which is okay with me. I was forced to talk in the hospital and that was enough for me. It was nice to not have to talk about it for once.

Any time I am forced to talk about it I find myself either 1) being a complete jackass or 2) apologizing for my actions. Which is actually quite insane if you ask me – apologizing for being suicidal. Oh yeah, my bad, it's like I chose to be this way. A lot of people just don't understand. Instead, they assume. Assume that we depressed people are just overreacting. Assume that we are throwing ourselves a pity party. Assume that we just want attention. Wrong, wrong, and wrong. News flash: I'm not overreacting and I don't want your pity, let alone my own. I just want a solution to the pain, and that solution just so happened to be suicide. Just imagine having suicide on your mind 24 hours a day, 7 days a week. It's like death is knocking at your door, but you're trying so hard not to let him in. I didn't ask for this. I don't know why these thoughts dance around my head all day and night. It's a terrifying thing to feel this way and not know how to stop it.

For my sister, I think this situation has been extremely difficult. When we were younger, one of her close friends committed suicide and I know that it still saddens her to this day. She is one of the strongest people I know, but suicide is one thing that really shakes her up.

One memory that is forever etched in my mind was seeing her leaning over me when I overdosed the summer before my senior year in high school. Her facial expression was filled with fear and her body language was frantic. She was crying and kept trying to keep me from dozing off. I was sprawled out on our family room floor and, in that moment, it felt like time had stopped. I vividly remember my sister above me telling me how much she needed me to hang on. She kept telling me that she couldn't lose me. On my other side, I remember her husband checking my vitals and encouraging me to keep my eyes open. We may be completely different people, but damn, do I love them.

My brother-in-law lost his brother not too long ago so death is really not a friend of his and my sister's. For that reason, I think dealing with my suicidal ideations has been especially hard for them. My brother-in-law sat me down and spoke to me about how he has coped with some dark times of his own. If there is one person who knows dark times, it's him. Between the loss of his brother and being deployed overseas, he has demons of his own that he has had to face in the past. We've never really had conversations like this before, but I'm glad he went out of his comfort zone to connect with me.

To my surprise, I feel safe here, and loved. I wish that I could stay here instead of having to drive back home.

Jay and I took the girls into the city today with one of our friends who lives downtown. They were excited to get out of the house for the day, even though it was freezing outside. Jay is so good with them and I find myself smiling due to the smiles on their faces. He has always played a positive role in my life and I'm glad the kids seem to love him just as much as I do.

Jay's positivity lights up the room anywhere we go. I guess you could say he is like a modern day hippie because he always has such great perspective toward the world and people in general. I honestly cannot imagine having embarked on this journey without him by my side. He always knows the right thing to say — even when the right thing is nothing. Most importantly, he hasn't given up on me yet. He has stood by me on my darkest days and still chooses to love me day in and day out. Talk about a good friend.

His and my friendship go way back to middle school. We met in one of our classes and immediately hit it off. At one point, he and I even "dated." He has always been there for me. From broken hearts to family problems to surgeries. He has never left my side, he has never judged me, and he has never stopped loving me. I used to sneak out in the middle of the nights in high school and run to his house just to sit with him in silence. We didn't even need to say anything. He just understood. He knew every inch of my mind and how it was constantly fighting off dark thoughts. He knew every inch of my heart and how it longed to love and be loved. He just knew me for everything I was, and he still knows me for who I am now. His friendship is a lifeline that continually keeps me afloat when I feel like sinking.

Despite the amount of fun I've had spending time with Jay and the kids, I can't help but to feel sad still. My nieces and nephew provide me with so much joy, but it is only short lived. If they can't provide me with everlasting joy, then what will? I'm scared to go home tomorrow. I'm not sure if I'm ready to face disappointment – from my family, from my friends, and from myself. I have always been the independent one in the family, but now what am I? Sometimes I wonder if the pressure to be so independent and "perfect" drove me to this cliff in the first place.

I've only been home for a few days, but it's already been too long. I've barely moved from my bed the past 48 hours. I think everyone assumed this would be the best option for me because I would be surrounded by family and friends. What they did not account for was their busy schedules and long spans of time when I would home alone. Both of my parents work all day and my brother has school and soccer in the evenings. Therefore, that leaves me in an empty house for about 75 percent of each day during the week.

I spend most of my day in bed. My headphones rarely leave my ears during the day and sometimes at night as I fall asleep. It gives me a way to drown out the world, including my own thoughts. My thoughts dissipate as the beats take over and my mind is temporarily shut off. I know my mom gets annoyed that I would rather lay in bed with my headphones on than come downstairs. In my defense though, it's not like anyone has actually tried to talk to me about what happened.

Ever since I got home everyone has pretended like nothing happened. It's like no one acknowledges the fact that a week ago my life could have been over and my existence on this earth shattered. Being home is enough to "save me" and help me heal in their minds. I'm so angry at the world. Why do they always think that it's an easy fix? It's not my environment that's causing my suicidal thoughts – it's much deeper than that. But the world doesn't like to treat the cause - just the symptoms.

Most people think that I'm healing from a bad break-up and I need to get over it. That's not it at all. Yes, it was painful and still is, but the break-up was just a trigger – not the underlying cause of my depression. Loss of my home. Loss of my job. Loss of my faith. Those are the real losses that I grieve over and led me to my sadness. No one sees any of that though. They just see the surface level and their superficial beliefs as to why I am the way I am.

I know that getting back into my work out routine will help lift my spirits, but I physically cannot pull myself out of bed. I feel weak, fatigued, and too lethargic to even open the blinds. My room stays dark most of the day because I refuse to let in any light from outside. I want to sleep and sink into my bed in hopes that a heavy sleep will make this all go away. I am in a black hole, unable to fight my way out. The good news is that I am aware of it, but now how do I find the light?

One positive step I have taken toward recovery is that I've stopped mixing medications. I know that's the best thing for my health, but now I'm completely vulnerable to any and every emotion. I'm swimming in these feelings of dark blue and each day the shades are only getting darker.

Trying to deal with these feelings won't get any easier either. I am supposed to start my graduate school classes online this week. Talk about impeccable timing. Idealize suicide attempts, get admitted to hospital, lose everything, move home, start over. Oh, and P.S., now you have to start classes. Not sure how the fuck I'm going to focus on classes at a time like this, but I hope I can get my shit together so I don't waste money that I don't have. Which is a whole different issue in itself – money. I still have bills to pay yet no income right now. I've started to look for jobs online, but haven't found anything for my profession. All this worry stemming from my lack of financial stability is making my life ten times more stressful.

In the meantime, I'm just going to take my anxiety medication and sleep this stress off. I just hope that the nightmares give me a break tonight.

Jay came over to literally drag me out of bed today. This has become a common routine these days. Most days I'm too tired to even get out of bed and let him in. When I say he literally has to get me out of bed, I'm not joking. He had to do some serious convincing to not only get me out of bed, but to put a change of clothes on and eat something before we headed to the gym. He is so patient with me. He is caring and kind. He is never quick to anger even when I'm acting like a total bitch. He's the only person who has made a complete commitment to helping me and it does not go unnoticed.

We started going to the gym every morning. I force myself to go with him, but I still have no motivation once I get there. I half-ass a few exercises and call it a day. That's better than nothing though, right? At least it gets me out of bed and out of the house for a while.

I haven't really spoken to many other friends since I've been home. No one has really made an effort to come see me, but that's mainly because I pushed them all away in anger. Some of my childhood best friends live down the street so it's nice to have them so close if I actually feel like getting out of bed that day. I'm just not ready to face the people who let me down yet. We are supposed to meet up later this week, but I'm nervous and scared. Nervous to tell them how disappointed I am, but even more scared that they will hate me when I do.

I met with my "best friends" today – the ones I was most scared to see. I can honestly say I have no idea where our friendships stand. I explained to them again how I felt and how serious the situation was. They still hadn't heard every piece of my story until now. I told them how disappointed and angry I was with them when they all made excuses for why they couldn't be there for me. I knew it would be a hard conversation, but I also knew that relationships are nothing without honesty. I couldn't move forward if I wasn't open with them. My actions were, by no means, their fault, but I do think a lot of the painful and traumatic events that followed could have been prevented if they stopped making excuses when I originally reached out for help. I tried to be as respectful as possible when having the conversation, but I didn't sugarcoat it either.

For the most part, they understood. They each reacted in their own way – some more understanding than others. I know that I hurt them too. They think I'm selfish for wanting to take my life and leaving them with that kind of pain. I can apologize for causing pain, but I cannot apologize for how I feel. I can't control my own feelings and thoughts right now. I will not say sorry for something I have no control over. As tough as the conversation was, I'm glad that we finally had it. These individuals have been alongside me from the beginning of my battle with depression. Despite the hostility we may feel toward each other right now, I know that our love for one another will mend this in time. I know that I can forgive them. I just hope that they can do the same for me.

On another note, my one friend I spoke to on the phone a lot when in the hospital invited me to join him at church. While I appreciate his effort to help me find Christ again, I don't know if I'm ready. I still have so much hatred in my heart. I am confused and haven't found any reason to believe that God exists. It's going to take me some time to even consider going down that path again.

Before I left my home in Arizona, I did something stupid (but what's new though). When my ex originally broke up with me he was more than kind and offered to help pay for some things to help me out during the transition process (moving costs, my own apartment, etc.). He was generous with his money – partly because he had a big heart and partly because he probably felt a bit guilty. Well, he gave me an inch and I took a yard. I definitely took advantage of his offer and my parents were furious. They didn't want me to accept anything from him or his family after everything that happened. I wrote a check to pay back a large portion of the money he lent me, but my parents think I should return all of it.

Honestly, I am so sick of them nagging me all the time. I know they just want what's best for me, but I think I can figure that out on my own. I still have a lot of negative feelings toward him and his family, so it's difficult for me to feel bad about accepting the money. It makes it a lot harder to be thankful for the help he offered long ago when he is no longer the kind person I used to know.

My parents and I have been getting into a lot of arguments lately due to this whole situation. My father told me how ungrateful I was because I don't appreciate all of the support they've provided me with since I've been back. I have been many things to them throughout my life, but ungrateful is the least of them. Throughout my life, appreciation and gratitude are the things I have been best at expressing toward my parents. I am not perfect, but I do know that I have always gone out of my way to show the appreciation and gratitude that I didn't always get in return from my parents and siblings.

His definition and my definition of support are completely different. He is referring to a roof over my head and a place to stay while I pick up the pieces to my broken life. The real support I need is emotional. I can't really blame him though. He has never been the type of father to sit down and talk about things like this. My mom is more of the emotional support in the family. I don't hold that against him, but I have always sought out my father's love, and this time isn't any different.

I have been lashing out on them and I'm ashamed of it. I have never acted this way toward them – absolutely disrespectful. There has been multiple occasions where I have cussed at them and I know that just makes my dad mad and my mom sad. I want help, but I just keep pushing them away in the process. I can see how heartbroken it makes my mother, and how frustrated my father feels. I don't know how to control it though. My anger has reached a whole new level recently which makes forgiveness an impossible thing to attain right now. I need to get a grip on my anger soon or I will lose everyone that I need to get through this.

Some good news (for once) is that I am going to Vermont with my best friend's family. His family is like my second family – a home away from home. I've never known a family that shows so much love and support to those around them. They have been nothing short of generous over the years while I dealt with my mental health issues. When I got home I quickly reached out to them because I knew they could help lift my spirits. After catching up over dinner, my best friend's parents immediately invited me to join them on their snowboarding trip up north. I know I have some things to mend at home, but spending some time with them sounds like a good way to clear my mind for a few days.

Something about being on the slopes, surrounded by the natural beauty of the outdoors and snow-white trees is absolutely breathtaking. The moment I stepped foot on the mountain, it's like everything was put on pause. The sadness. The worries. The anger. It all dissipated in that moment and all I saw was light. I saw hope for better days. It felt like I was taking my mask off and smiling with meaning for once. The fog that once clouded my mind cleared and I was able to find myself again – the me I had been searching so long and hard for.

The day was filled was fun and laughter, not to mention a lot of hot cocoa and quality time. My best friend and his brother rode the slopes with me while their parents spent some time down at the mountain resort. For the first time since this whole mess, I felt free. Listening to my music as I rode down the mountain, I couldn't help but smile ear to ear. It felt so good to break free of the darkness and shame. It was comforting to be able to enjoy something and not feel like I was pretending. Even after we got off the slopes and hung out with the whole family, I that warm feeling of happiness resided in my heart and mind the remainder of the night.

Being around my best friend and his family has brought me hours of laughter. I'm so thankful for their unconditional love. It has been two months since I've felt this type of joy. It's hard to believe that this is the time in months that I've been able to push the suicidal thoughts out of my mind. Without this trip, I'm not sure I could've found the light on my own.

Well, that glimpse of hope was short lived. We left Vermont today and I already feel myself sinking into dark blue. The worst part is feeling it coming, but not being able to do anything to stop it. It's like being on an airplane knowing it's about to crash, but there's nothing you can do to prevent it. You just brace yourself and hold on for dear life. I just don't understand how I can go from being so high to the absolute lowest in a matter of 24 hours.

I don't know how many times I'll have to fall back into this cycle. This is why it's almost easier to stay feeling low because then you don't get your hopes up just to be crushed again. Which is why I don't always put up a fight. Sometimes it's just easier to stay down. I know that sounds so bad, but my mind is constantly playing tricks on me. Any time I even start to think positive, I am reminded of the anchor that pulls me back to darkness. I don't know how to fight it and break free. I was hoping that the light I found in Vermont would follow me back home, but I am feeling more hopeless than ever. I am scared that I will never find my way out.

The one good thing about coming home from the trip was being with my dog again. This was the first time I'd been away from her since I was hospitalized. The idea of being apart from her makes me anxious and it gets harder to sleep at night. Having her by my side brings me a sense of comfort going into these lonely nights. She may not be able to understand what I say to her, but she understands my emotions and knows when I need her presence the most. Laying here next to her right now makes the darkness a little less lonely.

I finally forced myself to accept Rob's invitation to attend church with him. Although I can't say it was the best decision considering the outcome. The end result consisted of me bawling my eyes out in the middle of the service surrounded by people I'd never met before. When the worship music started, I looked around and saw joy in every person there. They were opening their hearts to Christ and I longed for that. Worship music used to make me feel so close to Christ, but all I felt was a sense of discomfort. It felt foreign and unknown to me.

I'm not even sure why I started crying, but once the tears started I couldn't stop them from flowing. I had to leave the room because I was so embarrassed. I felt so out of my comfort zone. More than anything though, I was filled with sadness. I envied what the other people in that room had – faith. I could see it in the way they danced, sang, and praised the Lord. But, for some reason, I couldn't feel even a tiny bit of that. Shame began to fill my heart because I was unable to accept Christ into it.

I'm sure I will be able to go back any time soon. I just don't understand why God won't show me how to believe again while I am over here searching so hard. It's not like I'm completely closed off to finding my faith again – I just haven't found a reason to believe in Him.

This girl got hired for a job and is employed again! It may only be part-time, but at least I will have something to look forward to each day. I've been going crazy (or some would say crazier) in my parents' house and graduate school classes aren't nearly enough to keep me busy. My new job isn't a dream job by any means, but at least it's better than nothing.

Things are getting a little better at home. I don't lash out as much and am trying to understand where my parents are coming from. Things are becoming "normal." It is becoming easier to get out of bed and finish my work outs. I haven't completely escaped my demons yet, but at least the movement is forward now. I no longer feel stuck in that wretched quick sand.

One thing I'm still having trouble with is finding my faith again. I'm trying to keep an open mind, but after my last church visit I am terrified to go back. I struggle with the questions in my head, but the biggest one remains – where is my God? At this point, it would just be nice to have something to believe in. Anything. I am going to start going to young adult groups at my friend's church. I think that may be a better approach than throwing myself into a full blown worship service again. It's hard not to be negative though. I'm trying my best to keep searching and seeking for something to believe in.

I can't tell you how or why it happened, but I felt so overwhelmed with God's love today. I was sitting in church like any other morning, but today felt different. Promising. The moment the worship music started I felt this sense of peace flow over me. It was like all the reassurance I had been looking for was finally right in front of me. I have been searching for some kind of sign these past few months – anything to keep me hanging on to hope. For the first time in months, I cried tears of joy. What I had been longing for these past few weeks had finally found its' way inside my heart again.

It's so hard to explain the feeling of Christ's presence to someone who has never experienced it. I'm not sure I even know how to begin to describe it, but it makes you feel vulnerable, and not the type of vulnerability that makes you scared. This is the type of vulnerability that breaks you down to build you up, and then empowers you to move mountains. It lights a fire in your soul and replaces every fear, doubt, and worry with strength, hope, and love. Every inch of me was overcome with peace. In that moment, I was made new.

The sermon message was something along the lines of learning how to stop blaming the world for all your pain and learning how to make the world better. I don't know why that was the sermon that spoke out to me so boldly, but at that moment I knew that I had the opportunity to share my story to help others. It was like everything clicked in my head and, instead of pitying myself, I decided to use my hardships to create change. I'm not really sure how or when, but I think I'm ready to help others that have dealt with similar issues as myself. I feel comforted knowing that I can create a new foundation on Christ again. I know it's only been one day, but I have a feeling the strength of my faith is only beginning.

Accepting Christ into my heart again was a great feeling, but it also challenges me on a whole new level. Learning to forgive myself and others that hurt me has been so difficult, but now I feel like I am held to a higher standard to achieve that forgiveness. I know that Christ forgives me for my sins, but why can't I forgive myself? It has become easier to forgive those who hurt me, but I am still so ashamed of myself that it feels impossible to allow myself grace.

Since I found Christ again, I have been struggling to accept the fact that a God-fearing man created so much pain in my life. I know that no one is perfect, but I did not expect God to put someone in my life that would claim to be His follower and then betray me. One thing I do know though is that my ex-boyfriend is a good person. What he did doesn't make him a terrible person, but he did make a terrible mistake (haven't we all?). Finding my faith again has helped me clear my head a bit and remind me that we are human. We are not perfect. We sin. We make mistakes. We live and we learn. That is what I pray for him now. I pray that he learns from his mistakes and the hurt he caused. I know that one day, when he is in a good place with Christ again, he will realize his mistakes and hopefully come to place of forgiveness. I won't wait around for an apology, but I have a feeling that he will come around if he sets his foundation on Christ again.

I tried to explain this to one of my friends, but all she has to say are negative things about my ex and his new girl. I still hold some sadness and anger from everything, but I have made a conscious effort to keep those emotions buried. I truly wish the best for him and try to see good in him despite everything. It makes me upset sometimes that my friend doesn't see the progress I made toward a more positive outlook. I don't think she realizes that her hateful words toward them just pull me back into a negative place. I know she doesn't understand where I am coming from when it comes to my forgiveness and faith, but I wish she would at least try. It's frustrating trying to become more positive when all she brings to the table is bitterness. I love her, but I think her approach to my healing isn't exactly what I need right now.

Learning how to love myself and find lasting happiness is one of the hardest things I've ever had to do. They don't teach you this stuff in school. Don't get me wrong – I've been pretty "happy" for the most part, but it's so hot and cold. One day I am ready to seize the day and other days I'm contemplating driving off a bridge. It's a work in progress, but I wish there was an easier way or a quick fix.

Traveling has made it easier to cope with everything recently. I've started planning more trips ever since I got back from Vermont. I'm not trying to run away from my problems, but it helps ease the pain while I'm still healing. I just got back from a visit to see one of my best friend's in Maine. She is one of the most positive influences on my life due to her upbeat personality. Very rarely have I ever seen her sad or upset because she always has a positive outlook on life.

What I love the most about her is her honesty and loyalty. She never fails to tell me as it is, but always has my back when I need her most. Despite our differences, she has always been understanding when it comes to my depression. She may not fully understand how it works, but she supports me just the same.

Back in college, she was one of the few teammates who really knew why I left team. Instead of judging me, she loved me for who I was. She was the one who was there for me after my college boyfriend cheated on me and helped pick up the pieces to my broken heart. She always stood by me when no one else would. She always chose the harder path of being my shoulder to lean on and never for one second did she make me feel like a burden. She was there when I cried, but also when I was at my highest highs, sharing laughter during fun nights downtown.

Looking back, it saddens me to reflect on how many people truly leave your side when the going gets tough. I know that depression and mental illnesses scare and confuse people, but that's no excuse to leave a friend or loved one behind. I have lost countless friends from this disease. I noticed it a little bit in high school, but really started realizing it in college. One of my best friends at the time also happened to be one of my roommates. She and I were inseparable throughout our first year of college. The moment I quit soccer and let the darkness in was also the moment I lost my friendship with her. There were a lot of other factors (because, let's face it, I'm not perfect either), but I know that my emotional outbursts were the end of her and I. It was too much for her, and I don't blame her for that. The same thing happened with one of my good friends when living in Arizona too. The burden of my demons was too heavy for her to carry and, just like that, another friendship bit the dust.

That's probably the worst thing about depression. Losing loved ones – friends, family, etc. It just gets too hard. For them. For me. It becomes more work to hold on to these relationships when I am at my most fragile. People will let you down. They always will. But I have also learned that I cannot always blame them or myself. I blame the disease. The darkness. The demons. The lack of control I have when it hits me head on. I need to get out of the mindset of expecting people to let me down. Instead, I need to learn how to love unconditionally and forgive them when it does happen. And most importantly, forgive myself.

As the weeks go by, forgiveness has been one thing that has gotten easier and easier. There is still a sense of anger toward those who hurt me, but I'm working on it. I still struggle to find it in me to forgive myself. The shame and embarrassment of my past haunts me each day and forgiveness seems like the last thing I deserve. Some days I hate myself. For what I've done, or tried to do, and the things I've said. For the people I've hurt, and continue to hurt. But then I remind myself I am not perfect and no time is too late to mend a broken relationship – even if it's with yourself.

Which, speaking of, I've been trying to do with my ex. And when I say mend a broken relationship I don't mean try to get back with him. I mean mending the brokenness of how we said our goodbyes (or lack-there-of). I want to make sure he knows how sorry I am. I want him to know how much my heart aches for the cold things I said to him and his now girlfriend. I wrote a letter consisting of heartfelt apologies and good wishes, and I can honestly say I meant every bit of it. He probably doesn't think I do which is why I still haven't gotten a response from him. Not that I really expect a response from him, but if the man I once knew is still in there then I know he would forgive me and apologize as well. But I can't sit around waiting for him to reciprocate those heartfelt apologies. I know no contact with him is probably for the best, but it doesn't make the healing process go by any faster. I truly care for him and, in the end, I hope he knows that in his heart. I want to believe that he still wishes the best for me too, but I can't hold my breath waiting around to find out.

I've been having some low days recently. I can't explain why, but they just happen. Sometimes I feel like I will never escape this feeling of dark blue. It sucks. Like, really sucks. You just feel so hopeless sometimes. But then I remember that my God will never abandon me. Through Him, my weaknesses become my strengths. So I pray, and hope for a better tomorrow. I read Psalm 143 over and over, and remember how I overcame the darkest days to get where I am today. It will never be easy, but at least I've got God on my side.

I literally can go from being super happy to absolutely hopeless in a matter of seconds. It doesn't make sense and I wish I knew how to stop it already. When it happens, I just want to isolate myself. There is nothing anyone can say or do to snap me out of the trance that depression pulls me into.

Today I spent some time outside before I finally gave in. I figured some fresh air would help snap me out of it, but no such luck. My bed acts as a safe haven at times – wrapped in my sheets with the lights down low. I close my eyes in hopes that the sleep carries me to brighter places.

I've been thinking a lot about how this all started. The depression. The anxiety. The suicidal thoughts. Was this all genetic? Was I doomed from birth? Or does our society cultivate environments that allow this dark culture to grow? I definitely think that mental health issues run in my family so I know that I could have been genetically predisposed to this disease. Except, the problem was that no one talked about it. My mom. My dad. My sister. No one warned me. No one helped me understand how to deal with this monster, or how to fight it. If only society didn't make us so scared to talk about it, then maybe I would've been more prepared walking into my battles.

Besides the genetic aspect, my environment definitely triggered some onset of depression throughout the years. Pinpointing the exact time is difficult though. I do know it stemmed from hateful words and bullying throughout high school and college. That's right. I said it. Bullying. The break-ups were heartbreaking, but what really broke my heart was the backstabbing friendships and cold-hearted people.

When I was in high school, I had it all. Literally. A roof over my head, a loving family, and a lot of great friends. I aced all of my classes and never let my GPA drop below a 4.0. I played varsity soccer all four years as well as club soccer, all while juggling a part-time job. And I was "popular" (relatively speaking). Most people knew me as the girl who wore a bright pink "virginity rocks" t-shirt my first few years in high school. Or the girl who played soccer. But it wasn't until my junior and senior year when they started seeing me in a different light. What happened? High school happened.

The hateful words started shortly after my boyfriend and I had broken up. Parties were planned and I stopped getting the invite because he was usually the one hosting them. Some of my best childhood friends started hanging out with him more and me less. I tried not to take it personally because I never wanted them to choose. But I did want support. For once, I wanted someone to stand up for me. Was I overemotional at times? Absolutely. But seeing everyone accept the fact that he treated me poorly really took a toll on me.

Eventually, I moved on and started talking to a new guy after being hesitant for a long time. My friends knew about him and encouraged it. So, it was to my surprise when I heard the news about them hooking up with him at a party my ex-boyfriend threw. My judgement in boys obviously wasn't the greatest, but I couldn't fathom the idea of my "best friends" doing such a thing. The worst part was that not only one, but THREE of them had hooked up or made out with him that night. I was crushed. This event cascaded into broken friendships and hateful words. Girls that I used to call my sisters were now spewing hurtful things behind my back while also making fun of me on social media. They would write things on social media where I could publicly see them mocking me and even laughed in a rude manner when I won homecoming queen my senior year. There were so many little things building up.

That's the thing though. The little things are not just little things. The little things chip away at your exterior and, next thing you know, they shake your core. I will never forget one night sobbing in the kitchen of my house. Those little things finally broke me that night. My parents were there listening to me as I kept telling them how I couldn't understand why my "friends" would be so mean. It didn't make sense to me then. It still doesn't makes sense to me today.

Thankfully, over the years, I had the opportunity to mend the broken relationships that hurt me throughout high school. There are really no excuses for bullying, but I will chalk it up to the fact that we were young and stupid.

Fast forward a couple of years to my freshman year in college. I had messed up badly, and badly is probably an understatement. I did something I never thought I would do – I cheated on my boyfriend. I don't believe in having regrets, but that is one thing I will always regret. Intentionally hurting someone who cares for you – probably the worst thing you could ever do. I'm not proud of it, and sometimes I even tell myself that's why I've been cheated on the last 3 years of my life – karma. I shamed myself, apologized, and moved on. Thankfully, this is the only ex-boyfriend who never hurt me and also found it in his heart to forgive me. However, others weren't as quick to forgive.

One of his close friends was a girl a couple years older than him (one grade above me). To say she hated me was an understatement. She was just being a protective friend though and I can understand that. I was in the wrong, but it was in the past and we had moved forward. When I reached out to her later in the year to apologize and clean the slate however, I got a response that quite literally made me want to kill myself.

Word for word, her message read statements such as:

"Bitch... I do not care about your apology... I would have accepted it if you weren't such a fucking slut."

"You are a piece of shit… you deserve nothing but the worst, you fucking slut."

"You're a waste of a fucking life."

I contemplated killing myself that night. Her words were etched in my mind and served as a constant reminder of my imperfections. I was worthless. I already felt like a piece of shit, and now hearing it from her confirmed it. I didn't need someone to tell me twice that I was a "waste of a fucking life" because I already felt that way about myself. I distinctly remember drinking and using inhalants frequently for the nights following those messages.

So, going back to how all this started… I don't think there was ever one real answer. It was genetics. It was my environment. It was my own mistakes. There are probably factors I still haven't figured out yet, but I do know that the things that can be controlled – like talking about it, educating society, and preventing bullying – need to be a priority. Maybe I can help others deal with their mental health issues better by tackling the very things that made mine worse.

I received some surprising news today and I'm not really sure how I feel about it. I found out that my ex and his girlfriend are going to have a baby. I don't follow anything online, but some of my friends messaged me this afternoon with the news. I would be lying if I said my heart wasn't fragile still, so I try to avoid seeing anything that might trigger any negative feelings. I almost wish my friends wouldn't have sent me the picture of their pregnancy announcement, but I know I would've seen it sooner or later.

When I first received the news that she had moved in with him, along with her children and their new puppy, I was outraged. It was less than a month and half after I had moved back to the east coast, and I was nowhere near ready to see his life transition from me to her. He and I had picked the house out together and it felt like a knife to the back knowing he was now sharing it with her.

Today has been weird though because I don't really know how to react. I thought it would put me into that place of dark blue, but I feel relatively okay right now. Am I sad? Yes. Am I a little angry? Yes. But honestly, what can I do? I have always seen pregnancy to be something beautiful, so a little piece of me is happy. Happy to see something so beautiful come out of something so tragic. I have reached a point where I am glad to see him doing well, but I would be lying if I said it didn't sting. This was our plan – our future. I was supposed to be the one talking about marriage and creating a family with him. It's hard to transition from having those discussions with him to seeing him carry it out with another woman within a matter of months. Regardless though, it is what it is, and I wish them the best despite the circumstances.

I feel like all the pieces are finally falling into place for me. Today, I signed the lease on my own apartment with a new roommate. I am FINALLY moving out of my parents' house. I am appreciative of being surrounded by my family, but I can honestly say that this is the final piece I needed to feel independent again. Signing the lease today reminded me that I can pick myself up and start over no matter how long or difficult it seems.

The freedom of living on my own again is so refreshing. Being financially independent is something that I have always strived for, but this process was pretty tough. Going from practically having nothing and relying on others for support to being able to take care of yourself is a great feeling. I think my pride hurt more than anything to accept help from my parents during these past few months. I hope I can use this time to make up for that and repay them for everything they've done for me.

My roommate and I started going to a church near our new apartment. First off, my roommate and I get along so well which makes living together a piece of cake. I really love that she shares a love for Christ like I do and accepts me for all my flaws. One of our coworkers invited us to their church and we immediately fell in love. It feels good to be a part of something bigger than ourselves – a part of a community.

Something I have been searching for lately is community. Don't get me wrong, I have plenty of family and friends I love to be around and share experiences with. However, ever since I accepted Christ into my heart again, I noticed the lack of faith-based friends I have in my life. It is tough to stay walking a straight line with Christ when you have no one walking beside you. I have really been trying to surround myself with fellow believers because I know that they can help me stay on that path. That doesn't mean I love my other friends any less, but the ones who understand support me.

One of my childhood best friends who grew up on the same street as me is also a Christian. I am beyond grateful for her presence in my life. She knows my deepest, darkest secrets and has chosen to love me despite them. Her encouragement is continually pushing me in my walk with Christ and lifting me up when I fall down. Her and I have been through our fair share of troubled times over the years and our relationship is far from perfect. Which is what makes it so beautiful. Our imperfections make us who we are and I wouldn't change our relationship for the world. These are the types of relationships I long for now. Genuine, faith-based, and forgiving. Without them, it would be a lot harder for me to stay afloat during the storms.

Well, today really blows. I just got home from an awesome trip down to my friend's cabin yesterday and today that buzz was immediately killed when my boss called me in to fire me. I called out for an emergency and missed work for the first time since being hired there 3 months ago, and now my boss was saying that he didn't think it was a good fit. I had busted my ass for this company completing new projects to help the business. I had come to love my work at the clinic, even if it wasn't my dream job. I was furious at him. Confused and embarrassed, I had never been fired before and I wasn't sure what to do next. I had honestly been looking for other jobs – something I was more passionate about – but I wasn't ready for this to happen.

I just rebuilt my entire life and don't really have time to sink back into a self-pity party. I cried for a little while and then snapped myself out of it. If I could get through this past year, then I could definitely get through this. I'm not going to lie though... my anxiety is out of the roof right now. I have bills to pay and I don't have much money saved up right now. Although I'm still working with some other companies through contracts, that income won't be nearly enough to pay for rent and everything else.

Any other time in my life, this probably would have destroyed me. It would have pushed me back into a corner and led me to that dark place I try so hard to stay away from. But in this phase of my life, it isn't affecting me as much as I thought it would. I'm stressed, yes, but I have this sense of calm knowing that God has my back. I know it sounds silly, but I have this feeling He has something great in store for me. I've worked too hard this past year just to end up here.

Talk about the best birthday ever. I just got off the phone with a guy from a professional sports team on the west coast. I had applied to a position with the team a few months back, but honestly thought I had no shot at actually getting it. Not to mention, I hadn't heard anything back for over month after applying for the position. Well, to my surprise, I got offered an interview and the position! I seriously can't believe this is happening. My life was in shambles at the beginning of the year and now look at it.

The best part about getting the phone call today was getting to share the great news with some of my best friends. I am in Charleston for my birthday weekend with some of my closest friends and I couldn't think of a better way to celebrate than on my birthday with them. One of my friends and I sat in the room crying tears of joy after the phone call. She knew how difficult my journey had been this past year and she knew how much I needed this position. It also helps that she shares a love for soccer like I do and knows how awesome this opportunity really is. Today I witnessed one of the best things that I will ever experience in life – getting to share a moment of pure joy with someone who also understood my moments of darkness. I knew the big man upstairs had something in store for me all along.

I can't say my parents are thrilled about this new job offer I got. I know they are proud of me, but the last thing they want is for me to move across the country again, but this time alone and knowing no one. After what happened the last time I moved across the country, they aren't necessarily encouraging me to go. They also think it is a bad idea financially. I won't be making a lot of money if I accept the position and the moving costs will practically force me to start from scratch once I get out there.

I know that my parents just want what is best for me and they think that turning down this offer and staying close to friends and family will be best. In the end, they said they will support me either way, but it makes me question my decision to accept this offer and move 3,000 miles away on a scarce amount of money.

For most of my life I have done the practical thing. I've always made the decisions that would be best for me financially and would "make sense." But, now, I don't want to play it safe. I want to follow my dreams. I'm terrified to make this move, but something about it has grabbed my attention and I can't quite shake it. I haven't been tested with a busy work load recently, but if I pick up another job to make ends meet then I will be working crazy hours and trying to juggle classes online. It sounds like a really bad choice considering how hard this new change could hit me. I can see why my parents would be worried... but I'm not sure I can put my dreams on hold any longer. I put my personal goals and career on the backburner for so long with my ex. Maybe it's time I make a decision and do something for me for once.

Well, I accepted the position and I officially move across the country the day after Christmas! This is all so exciting, but scary at the same time. I don't know anyone that lives in the area that I am moving to and the idea of having no support system there leaves my parents feeling uneasy. I won't lie – I feel the same way. I have grown independent again and stronger than ever, but you never really know when a low will hit and when you'll need your loved ones to lean on.

The best part about moving to a new place and knowing no one is that no one knows your past. The worst part about it though is also that no one knows your past. I'm really scared to open up to anyone about this past year because people either get scared, think I'm crazy, or get judgmental. I want to leave my past in the past though, so moving there will give me a fresh start. A clean slate is exactly what I need after these past 10 months.

It is days like today that I feel grateful for a God that is always looking out for me. In a matter of 24 hours, I locked in a place to live in California and another job that just so happens to make up for the lack of financial stability I have been stressing out about. I have been extremely proactive trying to get my life together, but some things are beyond my control. I can't help but to be thankful for all the things that have fallen into my lap recently.

However, when it comes to God and my faith, I have still been struggling to understand the purpose of this past year's events. I feel blessed to have made it out of what seemed to be the darkest period of my existence, but I can't help but wonder why He would make me endure that. I know people say "what doesn't kill you makes you stronger," but damn, I don't want to be on the verge of death to gain strength. I came close to dying multiple times at the start of this year, but I can't say I would want to go through it again just to come out a better person. I really have been struggling with this concept of God never giving us more than we can handle. I couldn't handle depression when I was at my lowest and I often question my faith knowing that God let it happen. I know many people probably struggle with that question, but I never know how to answer it when defending my faith. I can't defend my faith sometimes because even I don't know why He would let me feel that much pain.

I did come out stronger, smarter, and more positive, but I would never wish that journey on anyone. Maybe one day I will understand, but for now I'm just going to push it to the back of my mind. There may be a lot of things I don't understand when it comes to my faith, but the one thing I do know is that finding mine again was the reason I decided to fight – the reason I decided to live.

Moving day is finally here. I am about to embark on a cross-country road trip by myself (and my dog of course). While the first half of the year seemed to drag by, looking back, I feel as if it all happened in the blink of an eye. So many emotions in one year. So many tears, yet so much laughter. Depending on the way it's looked at, it could be interpreted as the worst year of my life or the best one yet. I almost gave up on life, but at the same time I learned how to conquer the demons that weighed me down.

I can't help but think how different my life would be if none of it ever happened. I would probably still be following someone else around, trying to help them reach their dreams while suppressing my own. I would still be the same loving person I am, but would not have learned how to love myself. I would have cruised through my days, but would not have learned how to overcome the darkest ones. I would have been comfortable, but would have never challenged myself to grow.

There are so many "what ifs" that cross my mind as I look back into the year. One thing that is for certain is that I can never stop loving myself. The moment I stop having love and faith in myself is the moment I begin to fail. This process of finding myself, finding my faith, and learning how to be positive was not, and still isn't, easy. This process is a journey that I will embark on for the rest of my life. I would like to think that the worst is in my past and that I can overcome any curveball that life tries to throw at me, but you never really know. Depression is an enemy of mine and I know that the war isn't over, but I can honestly say that the victor of this battle was me.

I cannot say I am happy to have faced the challenges I did over the past 12 months, but I am grateful to be alive. I am grateful for another chance at my pursuit of happiness. I am grateful for another chance at loving myself. I am grateful for another chance at life. I'm not sure what the future holds, but I am sure that it will be nothing like my past. I know that I cannot go back and create a new beginning, but I do know that I can make a new ending.

"Sometimes you get to what you thought was the end only to find it's a whole new beginning."

- Anne Tyler

I wrote this book and shared this story with you all for multiple reasons. The first being to raise awareness for mental health issues and everything that it encompasses – the broken mental health systems, the prescription drug problems, the stigmas, and, most importantly, the real monster behind the sad and anxious faces you may see throughout your lifetime. Mental health awareness and suicide prevention has made strides in recent years, but there is so much more we, as a society, can do. Often times, those affected by these diseases are too fragile and weak to be the voice we need to make change. So, this is me asking for your help to get involved. Eliminate stigmas on those who suffer from mental health issues. Make your voice heard to change public policies in our health system. Or simply provide a shoulder to lean on when someone is in their darkest hour.

The second reason I shared this story is to give you hope. There are times in each of our lives that we experience pain, sadness, and loss. We hit rough patches and some days it may take our strongest efforts to get by. I am living, breathing proof that these dark days can turn into the brightest tomorrows. I have been there, on the edge, in the darkness of a tunnel that feels never ending. But, here's the good news – YOU will see better days, YOU are strong, YOU are enough, and YOU will prevail. There are so many beautiful reasons to live and sometimes we just need a gentle reminder of them.

Finally, I felt like this story was an opportune time for me to share my journey from being a believer to a nonbeliever and back. I have been exposed to many things over the years that have helped me bounce back from depression, but my faith has been my saving grace. There are some things you just can't explain and the presence of Christ in my life has been quite the miracle. To not believe in anything and absolutely reject the idea of God, and then to be overcome with His love and strength during my darkest times left me awestruck. This feeling and relationship with Christ is something I hope all of you get to experience in your lifetime.

I want to thank everyone who has been a part of my journey these past few years. Those who were by my side every day and those who might have just been there for one day. No matter how big or small your part, you played an important role in my story and, ultimately, helped save my life. I would especially like to thank my family and friends for everything you had to endure while I found myself again. Your patience, love, and support will never be taken for granted. For you, I am forever thankful.

49492108R00071

Made in the USA
San Bernardino, CA
26 May 2017